Wakefield Press

SNOW IN THE SKY

Gina Inverarity grew up in South Australia and worked for many years as a book editor. Her first children's book, *The Brown Dog*, was published in 2017. *Snow*, her first young adult novel, and the first in this series, was published in 2020.

Praise for *Snow*

'Snow's voice drew me in deep from the very first page and held me fast until the end. An evocative, powerful story full of heart and spirit.' – Juliet Marillier, author of the *Warrior Bards* series

'Dark, enchanting and visceral. A classic fairytale brilliantly reimagined for our rapidly changing world.' – Margot McGovern, author of *Neverland*

'Snow is a captivating character; the writing is evocative and the book is a tactile and visual delight. Five stars.' – Katharine England, *Advertiser*

'One of the best young adult adventure stories published in a long time.' – Erich Mayer, *Arts Hub*

'*Snow* ... will no doubt be regarded as one of 2020's best YA novels.' – Joy Lawn, *Paperbark Words*

'Inverarity has pulled a thread from a great tapestry of storytelling and used it as the warp for weaving something entirely new.' – Catherine Norton, author of *Hester Hitchins and the Falling Stars*

SNOW IN THE SKY

⟵ ⟪ GINA INVERARITY ⟫ ⟶

Wakefield
Press

Wakefield Press
16 Rose Street
Mile End
South Australia 5031
www.wakefieldpress.com.au

First published 2025

Copyright © Gina Inverarity, 2025

Edited by Maddy Sexton, Wakefield Press
Cover illustrations by Sam Cowley
Typeset by Jesse Pollard, Wakefield Press

ISBN 978 1 92304 279 7

A catalogue record for this
book is available from the
National Library of Australia

Wakefield Press thanks
Coriole Vineyards for
continued support

For the trees

Glossary

afore	(now, soon)
anon	(soon)
art	(are)
aye	(yes)
be'est	(be)
canst	(cannot)
dint	(didn't)
dost	(does)
doth	(do)
ere	(before)
forswear	(lie)
f'r	(for)
hadst	(had)
hast	(has)
hath	(have)
hither	(here)
int	(isn't)
is't	(is it)
mine/mine own	(my)
nay	(no)
o'er	(over)
peradventure	(perhaps, possibly)
prithee	(pray thee, please)
t'feeleth	(that feels)
thee	(you, singular)
thou	(you)

thither	(there, toward)
thy	(yours, singular)
'twas	(it was)
wast	(was)
wee'ns	(children)
wend	(go in a specified direction)
whence	(where)
whither	(to which place)
wilt	(will)
ye	(you, plural)
yond	(more distant/over there)

Prologue

I sat slumped in the belly of my basket, alone but for the hawklet. The lines of my balloon creaked and the silks flapped, stiff with ice. It were calmer, I noticed. The storm had passed. It had been fierce and short. Though maybe I'd just been spat out on the other side of it like a bad taste.

I opened my eyes, my lashes heavy with icicles. I'd never been so cold on land as I felt now in the sky. Even frozen earth held warmth that a clear sky did not.

Where were my friends? Where was the hunter, Dog-boy, Rose Red? Had they been swept up into the heavens and lost? I peered over the frayed edge of my basket but the air was pale blue and as empty as a hollow heart. My chest hurt and it was hard to breathe which meant I was very high, probably grazing the very top of the sky.

Lady the hawklet regarded me from her perch in the bow. She spread her wings, poised to take flight. To leave me.

'I need to move. I know,' I told her croakily.

It was one thing to set my mind to it, it was another to make my limbs do as I asked. Frozen to the bone, moving was agony. My skin was tight and burnt by wind and sleet, my tongue swollen to twice its size for want of water. I pushed myself to sitting in the stern of the basket and grasped the wing trimmer. If it wasn't broken there was hope yet.

One thing at a time. I tried to remember what I'd been taught.

When I pushed the lever, I felt the basket turn in response.

All well and good, Lady seemed to say, as she adjusted her balance. *But where are you going?*

The sky behind us was black with rolling clouds. The sky ahead clear.

'Away from the storm, Lady. That's the way open, that's the way we'll go. For now.'

PART I

The mountain chateau

>>———>

It weren't me who opened the sky. I dint even die and come
back to life, although everyone thought I did. I rose from my
coffin and the clouds parted and we all saw the sun and the
stars for the first time since the clouding over. But that break
did not hold. Within months the clouds closed over, the sun
was lost and the cold wrapped around us once again. Then the
sea froze, not just close to land but as far as a person could
walk. I heard, though I did not see, that waves were frozen
mid-break all along the coast.

Our island became trapped in a frozen ocean.

News of hard times in the city came up the mountain on the
lips of those who made the trip. They started walking up from
the city and coming in through the chateau gates, arriving every
day. They carried their belongings and dressed in all the clothes
they owned against the cold, so they looked like a parade of
paupers and players. They were all hung about with coats and
babies, washtubs, harps, tents, scarves caught by the wind, spare
boots, crates of chickens, and dogs running alongside donkeys
pulling bicycle-wheel carts. I even saw a piano being pulled in
such a way. Once they'd passed through the chateau gates and

put down their things in the bailey they asked to see me. I hurried down from my bedroom, slipping my feet into unlaced boots, hair falling loose down my back and face still puffy from sleep. I thought they brought news of trouble but what they wanted was to ask me to open the sky again. I were confused, being awoken from sleep and by what they were saying.

All I did, years ago now, was get shot through the chest with an arrow, get very cold and then warm up slow. I tried to explain it to them. *I were never dead, just sleeping a deep sleep. The hunter had covered me in furs and the birds sang me up out of a frozen slumber.*

When I'd woken up the clouds parted and the sun appeared, weak and distant, as if behind a veil of some sort. The night sky were there as well. An infinity of impossibly distant stars, themselves all suns, as I'd been told, some appearing sharper than others, those further away like a glowing furry fuzz across the sky. A sky that people had forgotten were there.

I had nothing to do with the clouds parting, but people see what they want to see. If two things happen close together it's people's nature to see a connection between them. In the years following, they'd come to believe that I had opened the sky.

Following the short glimpse of the pale blue above the clouds, an even deeper cold settled over the island. That was when people started coming to ask me to clear the clouding over again. Their lives had become an unbearable struggle. It became a burden I could not put down.

'How'm I supposed to open the sky again?' I asked the hunter.

He shrugged. 'They think that seeing as you did it once, you can do it again.'

I frowned at him. 'You know I dint really do it the first time though, don't you?'

The hunter shook his head and looked embarrassed. 'It were a magical thing to witness, Snow. You don't remember it well. You being you, and having the touch with the forest and the birds, whatever gift it is that you have, I can't explain it. But it really appeared like you'd risen from your coffin and opened the sky. You can see how much it looks like you did, can you not?'

I looked at him like he were cracked in the head and went to milk the goats. Me banging in their pen and yanking on their udders upset them and they shifted restlessly, bumping the bucket. I put my palm to a doe's flank and calmed her. I reminded myself of the shelter and comfort in the stone walls that rose around us. There was fresh needle thatch on the roof of the goat shed, still smelling like sharp pine, keeping the ground dry and the herd warm. The walls were topped with fresh mortar and slate, the yards swept clean of snow soas the paths dint get people's boots muddy and mess up Cook's floors. The gardens were sealed in glass and warmed by fires kept burning on all but the mildest of days. The cellars were well stocked with sacks of root vegetables and shelves of preserves. Once or twice a season we took Cook's goat cheeses to the city and traded for the medicines and fuel we couldn't make ourselves.

In the city, so I heard, crops not grown under cover had started freezing and all the animals had to be moved inside. Bigger sheds were built, some of them out of ice, because why not? It was all around. There were hardly any trees left near the coast that hadn't already been burnt or sawn up. The cows dint seem to mind living in ice boxes and their milk started flowing again. So long as there was cow dung there could be fires to heat the greenhouses, but those without coin to pay for food grown indoors went without. Fox's city wasn't arranged in the same way as our chateau. There, if you didn't earn coin, you didn't buy food. At the chateau, all we asked is that people work for the good of all, and they could expect a bed and a meal and a life in return.

A watch was kept from the chateau towers day and night. This at the hunter's insistence. He said it was to spot game wandering close by, but really it were to keep a check on people coming and going. Counting heads, making sure everyone who went out through the gates were accounted for, and a search sent out after them if they dint appear back when they should. He weren't over his shame about leaving people to freeze outside all those years ago and now he was set on looking after those he could.

More city people arrived, chilled to the bone and exhausted from the long climb up the mountain. We gave them warm porridge and sat them around the fires in the bailey, and it became part of my morning to pass among them on my way to milk the goats. I took pains to explain that I weren't responsible for parting the clouds.

'It were a coincidence,' I said, again and again. 'That's all. But I can see how it looks,' I'd finish weakly.

I was met with blank stares. The older women sometimes looked at me sadly which I dint understand. It was like they felt sorry for me, when they were the ones with toes frozen solid and lips blue with cold, crying children around their legs. I asked Cook to find them beds and hoped not too many more would come. It were hard enough to keep everyone fed, though none could be turned away. We'd learned that the hard way.

The hunter wore himself ragged between hunting game and tending crops, determined no one would go hungry. Every twilight he left the chateau with his long stride to check no one were shut outside the gates who could still make it up the road before dark fell.

There came a morning when my tongue lay heavy in my mouth and I couldn't form the words of my usual speech about coincidence and me being nothen special. That day and all the ones since, I just welcome those arrived, holding people's hands and listening to their stories.

Just lately I stopped to pat a huge golden dog with a broad brow and drooping jowls. A boy sat by him wearing a patch slung over his right eye with his fingers dug deep in the dog's scruff, just like I used to do on my bear.

He frowned at me. 'Are you the Little Queen? You look like a plain girl.'

It weren't the usual thing people said. I'd grown used to my hand being kissed and pressed, people begging me to do the trick again. I'd started to believe that maybe I could. That maybe I should climb up on the east tower and raise my hands above my head. The mister teacher could give me a poem to say, something dramatic. I could get Little Bear to come and roar at the sky. See what happened then. Perhaps that would satisfy all these people coming up the mountain. Seeing some magic. But I was no actor.

I lifted my chin, flipped my long braid over my shoulder and placed my hand on my knife. 'My name is Snow and I *am* a plain girl,' I told the boy.

My nickname, Little Queen, had always made me uncomfortable. Used by some it were affectionate and by others it were mocking. Since I'd always had it, I never knew who'd given it to me or why, except that sometimes I could be bossy and order others about in a way that I always regretted after.

I changed the subject. 'You just arrived?'

The boy shifted from sitting on one foot to the other. 'Yes, miss. I came to see the queen who lifted the clouds.'

'What's your name?'

'I don't have one. Not that I remember.'

'How old are you?'

'Older than I look, being small for my age.'

'Who's your family?'

'All dead, far's I know.'

'I'm sorry to hear that,' I said. 'What happened to your eye?'

'Born that way. Gave my mama the spooks, people said, so she ran away from me.'

I felt for the boy, all alone. I knew that feeling. 'You're welcome to stay here if you're willen to work,' I told him.

'And my dog?'

'Does he bite?'

'Never has so far.'

'Then he can stay too. But he's not to chase chickens.'

The huge dog turned his ears back, offended. I were reminded of a dark night long ago when a dog just like him saved me from something awful.

'Poke never even noticed a chicken, miss.'

I smiled. 'Go and see Cook. She'll give you some boots and a coat and set you a task.'

The dog-boy hopped to his feet and set off in the direction

of the kitchen. It weren't hard to follow the smells of baking and frying.

He glanced back and turned, walking backwards over the uneven paving. 'Why's this house called the *chat-oh*?'

'That's what it's always been called. My father told me it's a word from an old language. It means house. But liken a *big* house.'

'It's big. Bigger'en any house I've ever seen,' the dog-boy said. 'They were right about one thing, miss. You are holden up the sky one way.'

Most days, after the midday meal, the children in the chateau gathered in my father's library for lessons. They spent their mornings helping with chores, and some were obliged to return to work after their lessons, but I'd made it a condition of staying that those with children send them to learn to read and write for those few hours.

The books in the library had not fared well during the long years when I were away and my stepmother was neglecting the old house. A hole in the roof had leaked snow and ruined the floor, and damp had crept up the shelves. By careful efforts of drying we saved many that had become waterlogged, and though their pages were bloated and puffy now, most of the type and pictures were still readable. I liked to look in on the school room as I went about my work, but not because it were always a picture of serenity: most of the time I went to check that the children had not chased the teacher under a table to torture him with dead silverfish, of which he had an unnatural fear. On those days, I were forced to growl and send the culprits to sweep the bailey as punishment and to make the trembling mister teacher a cup of tea to calm his nerves.

He was a slight man who'd left the city as a refugee after getting into trouble over a paper he'd written. It had caused him to lose his job and his reputation. I hadn't asked him many questions as it weren't my place to judge. Being scared of bugs did not bode well for living with us but then again, he'd found the chateau and the library and a purpose, however much he disliked it, and I had better graces than to remind him to be grateful.

'I cannot stand children,' he complained. 'You understand that I taught in a university, don't you? My students were *adults.*'

'Then you'll be pleased to hear that all children eventually turn into adults,' I told him. 'You have only to wait.'

He raised a trembling hand to loosen his collar dramatically. 'I may not survive until then.'

'There's always crops to grow or wood to chop,' I said, offering him a way out, but he waved me away.

On passing by the library door I saw the dog-boy laid out on the floor, turning pages slowly. Evidently he could read. As I watched, the mister delivered a large pile of books to the boy's elbow, the subject of which I couldn't make out from where I spied.

'Thanks, mister,' the boy said.

I patted Poke where he lay on guard outside the door and went on my way.

Little Bear did not live in the chateau with us. She found living behind walls did not suit her and preferred to roam the mountains and forests as we'd once done together. But she had the knack of finding us when we were out hunting, sometimes pushing game in our direction. Once the kill was made she'd amble in and collect her share.

'Don't need your help, Little Bear,' the hunter grumbled at her. 'Been hunting for longer'n you've been alive.'

My bear and I laughed at him, me in a human way and her by raising her snout in the air.

'Quiet, both of you,' said the hunter, trying to stay grumpy.

Out in the forest, walking up and down mountains, I shed the weight of responsibility that had settled on my shoulders. The years had been hard and the days were always full of toil but I reminded myself that bellies were full and babies were fat. The sky was heavy and the cold never ceased but the seasons of growing and harvesting turned like a well-greased wheel. There were deaths but these came naturally, not from want or privation. And there were births both human and animal, the most joyous of events. I was proud of our work and relieved we'd found a way to live without turning anyone away, without causing the natural way of things to get out of balance.

And yet, there was grit in the grease. A scratch that felt familiar and caused a welling up of dread.

Why the cold had worsened was a mystery. The sea freezing over seemed to say that we were headed into even icier times. Maybe instead of hoping for spring, we should be preparing for a deeper cold. As I understood it, these cycles of freeze and thaw took place over much longer than a person's lifetime. Even more than as many grandmothers as you could count. Breaking the cold cycle was done slowly, taking centuries, longer. It was not to be broken by some magic sung up by a plain old girl.

Standing in the forest with my hand deep in Little Bear's scruff I saw clearly. It weren't the people coming to ask me to lift the sky again. They were ghosts of my own making. It weren't magic that lifted the sky, but something had. And maybe it could happen again. It were just a matter of finding out how.

I dint say anything to the hunter but he looked up from his butchering and caught my eye as these thoughts passed over my mind. I turned away quickly. He could always see what I were thinking, like it were written in words on my face. The time would come to share but it weren't just yet. There was no need to tell him what I dint know myself.

But anyway, just then we heard the tower bell. Three tolls in quick succession. It were an alarm. Without a word, the three of us turned for the chateau and started running through the deep snow.

The flying-machine crash

>>———➤

The gates opened for us as we approached. The gate sentry directed us to the east tower and we raced up the steps two at a time. At the top was the captain of the watch. He passed the binocs to the hunter but they weren't needed to see what had raised the alarm. A cloud of snow had been lofted, as sometimes happens in an avalanche, behind a ridge to the east and north.

'What happened?' I asked the captain.

He nudged a skinny fellow forward – the boy with the eye-patch who I'd last seen in the library.

'Never misses anything, even with only one eye,' the captain said, by way of explanation.

The boy spoke up. 'It were a flying machine, miss. Descended through the clouds very fast and crashed just there as you see by the snow cloud.'

I were incredulous. 'A flying machine? What'd it look like?'

'It happened so fast,' the boy stuttered. 'And it were soundless. It caught my eye but we're supposed to be scanning the treeline,' this with a glance to his captain. 'So I only caught a glimpse. Just a breath or two of time. It looked like a silver boat and it trailed—' the boy hesitated and once again looked to the captain.

'S'all right, boy,' the hunter said. 'Speak your mind freely.'

'Well, miss, it looked to be trailing ribbons. Kind of like the ones girls tie in their hair,' he finished, gulping.

'I dint see any flying machine,' the captain said scornfully. 'More likely the sky is falling.'

'The sky int falling,' I told him firmly.

I looked between the dog-boy and the hunter, who'd put the binocs back to his eyes.

'How far?' I asked him.

'A few hours, if we go light and fast.'

The day was well underway. 'Just you and me then.'

'Grab your gear, Little Queen. I'll be waiting.'

A few moments later we were passing through the gates. We carried hunting gear slung over our shoulders once again but were now also loaded with food Cook threw in a pack as I passed back through the kitchen.

'Stay safe out there, Snow. Keep your wits sharp,' she told me.

I bent to kiss one of her round cheeks. 'We'll be back afore you've noticed we're gone.'

We'd barely made it through the gates, the hunter in the lead, Little Bear behind him and me bringing up the rear, before we heard crunching and puffing come up behind us. It were the dog-boy and Poke, following the path we'd cut through the thigh-deep snowfall. The cold were such a shock that it made both of them sneeze.

'Uh-uh, no way, yous are not comen,' the hunter said, planting his rifle butt on his boot with emphasis.

'Comen where?' Dog-boy said, leaning an elbow on his dog and making a comical attempt to look casual. 'Poke and me just taken the air.'

'You tell him, Snow.'

I paused a moment. The memories came back to me every time I passed through the chateau gates and this time were no exception. That pitch-black night long ago when the hunter had taken me from my tower cell, on orders from my stepmother to get rid of me, preferably by removing my warm heart from my chest.

'Honestly,' I said to the hunter, 'am I in any position to refuse? Does this picture not bring to your mind a like situation? Some time when you were being followed by a shivering, pathetic creature who dint know her knife from her nelly?'

I could see the hunter had been expecting me to take his side.

I went on. 'So far as we know, this int a life-or-death situation. We're not running, not this time. The boy saw the crash and can come if he has a mind to.' Turning, I said, 'But no complaining, do you hear? I can't stand whining about the cold or sore feet.'

In answer, Poke swivelled his ears, whiskers pulled back. Dog-boy looked similarly offended. 'I'm insulted, to be honest, Miss Snow. Do I look like a complainer?'

The hunter, growing impatient, re-slung his rifle. 'I've already got a headache from all the talking. Let's get moving.'

The boy grinned and patted Poke.

We made an odd party of expeditioners: me and my bear, a one-eyed boy and his dog, and the hunter. It were a good walk to the crash site and we'd wasted time already, so the five of us pushed on to the treeline and then followed familiar hunting trails through the forest, heading uphill, up high. We'd cross the ridge, drop into the valley on the other side and then follow the river up the gully to the next ridgeline where we'd seen the snow cloud rising. This were all familiar territory for me and the hunter. We'd both lived in this country for many months and knew our way. But it'd been a while since I'd walked out fast, and my legs told me so. I'd been living behind walls for too long. I were grateful to stop and wait every wee while for the boy to catch up.

'Just waiting . . . for the boy,' I told the hunter when he raised an eyebrow at my puffing. I threw a handful of snow at him. Dog-boy caught up and then passed me, lifting his knees almost to his chest to clear the snow with each step. When it went up past his waist he took a handful of Poke's thick leather collar and let the dog drag him over the drifts. The dog dint seem to mind.

The mysterious visitor

≫⟶

We approached the crash site in the late afternoon. With his uncanny sense of direction, the hunter had brought us right onto it. It were open country, up high. The air was crisp and clear, the ground icy. As always the sky was thick with cloud, a weight no one thought to feel anymore. I bade Little Bear to hold her ground and Dog-boy and Poke crouched down beside her. The hunter and me approached slow. We couldn't see any movement.

What we could see was an object that looked like the old tin baths that sat on broken tiles in the chateau bathrooms. It were grey and hung about over the sides with straps and ropes. Spread out over the tussocks for several metres were the ribbons Dog-boy had described. Fabric, like silk, mostly white but seamed in places with visible stitching and patched here and there with grey.

My hand were at my knife and the hunter had his finger on the trigger of his rifle, barrel lowered, as we approached careful and slow and quiet. As we got closer I could see a propeller at one end of the bath, and what looked like a tiller. *Were it some sort of flying boat?* I wondered. Soon we were close enough to see inside and there, crumpled in the bottom, was a person, grey in the face with a bright slash of crimson blood seeping from their head. The hunter slung his rifle and we hurried forward. I lay my fingers on the person's neck, feeling for a pulse. On its head was a cap and goggles, which made it even harder to see what kind of a creature it was. Small enough to be a girl, I decided, but the hair sticking out from underneath a cap was long and white like an old woman's. The way she was folded up in the boat with her arms tucked in beside her reminded me of an injured bird. She wore a grey suit, top and bottom in one, joined in the front by a zipper, and covered in pockets and buckles.

'She's alive,' I said, feeling a slow but steady pulse.

I pulled a cloth from my pack and pressed it to the cut on her head that was slowly oozing blood. This prompted a groan.

'S'all right,' I said. 'You been in a crash.'

'Here, give her some water,' the hunter said, passing over a bottle.

I held it to the old woman's lips and she managed a few sips.

Dog-boy, Poke and Little Bear approached, startling the bird-woman, who pulled off her goggles and cap and scrambled to the far end of her bath.

'S'all right,' I told her again. 'We're friendly, all of us. No one's going to hurt you. I'm Snow and this is the hunter. That's Dog-boy, Poke and Little Bear, though she's not so little anymore.'

The bird-woman's eyes only widened more and more in alarm as I did the introductions.

'Do you . . . speak?' I asked her.

Haltingly, like her tongue was sticking to the roof of her

mouth, she said, 'I am Madame Eveline-Madeline-Marie-Adelaide, Official Aeronaut of the Restoration. Mine balloon' – here she looked about in distress – 'hast crashed.'

This being obvious to everyone, the hunter raised an eyebrow. I wrapped a hand around his forearm in warning.

'We're honoured to meet you Madame Eveline-Madeline . . .'

'Thee may address me as Memma or madame.'

I were grateful for this kindness at shortening what seemed like enough names for a whole family rather than one small woman.

'It's an honour to make your acquaintance, Memma,' I said, remembering my manners and holding out my hand. Memma extended her own and we shook. Her hand felt cold and light in mine. Without her cap and goggles I could see she had wide-set blue eyes, a small pointy nose and a sharp chin. Her face was wrinkled around the eyes and mouth but her movements were light and quick so I couldn't make out her age. I supposed it weren't easy to launch a body into the sky, so best it be small and light.

'Pleased to meet you, Madame Memma,' the hunter said. 'Now, enough talk. We need to get to some shelter, afore the light fails and we all freeze. Can you walk?'

Memma looked confused.

'*Walk*?' the hunter said, louder, like she were deaf.

'Nay, mine ankle,' she said, indicating that she couldn't put weight on it.

The hunter and I looked at each other, deciding what to do. Meanwhile Dog-boy were tinkering around at the bow of the boat, lifting the straps and giving them experimental tugs. Memma glanced at him anxiously.

'With care!' she said.

Dog-boy stood. 'Poke can pull her,' he said. 'The whole kit don't look like it weighs much more'n me,' he said, giving it a shove.

'Ah! Nay, nay!' Memma said, again waving him off weakly. 'Please keep care! This is a craft of fine instruments. It canst be treated roughly.'

Dog-boy raised his eyebrows. 'You talk funny, lady. Where're you from?'

'Time enough for get-to-know-yous when we're all warm and dry, Dog-boy. Now, how about getting Poke hitched if you think he'll do it,' the hunter said.

With a whistle, Poke was summoned and backed up to the craft where Dog-boy slipped and tied the bath straps to Poke's collar and around his chest, creating a harness-like fastening. All the while Memma fluttered her hands, repeating, 'Be'est careful, young sir!'

The hunter followed the silks back across the snow field, gathering the fabric into his arms, taking care not to snag it. Bringing it back, he bundled it around Memma's legs, tucking the lines in neatly.

'Hold on, madame,' Dog-boy said. And to Poke, 'Come on, fella, easy.'

As the lines tightened, the boat moved a little and then slid over the snow, gently bumping. Memma whimpered a little, but I weren't sure if she were concerned for her craft or her injuries.

Late in the evening we reached a hut that would give us shelter for the night. It were one of the more broken ones of those left scattered in the high country. A hole in the roof had made a pile of snow on the floor, and the glass of the windows was long gone. But the stone chimney stood, the hearth cold but soon to be burning a fire to warm us all through. Poke pulled the flying machine up and the hunter bent and lifted Memma from where she lay wrapped in her silk ribbons. She had been dozing but woke up and looked about as he laid her in the hut.

While Dog-boy and the hunter found sticks and fuel to start a fire, I indicated Memma's ankle. 'Can I look?'

It took a moment for my meaning to make itself clear. It seemed we spoke the same language but in very different ways. She nodded and helped me unfasten the catches and buckles of her flying boot, wincing as I drew it free. Her ankle was swollen and looked painful but no bones broken, in my opinion. I wrapped it firmly in cloth.

'Thank thee, it feeleth much better,' she said, which I understood.

With the fire roaring we shared some of Cook's bread and cheese.

Dog-boy asked again as he fed Poke some dried meat, 'Where you from, madame? How come your bath fell from the sky?'

''Tis a balloon, young sir. And not a bath, a basket. I am a scientist-aeronaut, exploring the outer edges of the Restoration and gathering data on the orders of King Augustus the Third.'

'Did she say king?' Dog-boy asked, his forehead creased in his efforts to understand Memma's odd way of talking. 'Any relation of yours, Little Queen?'

Memma looked sharply at me.

'Aye! Art thee queen?'

'Dog-boy, for the love of Little Bear!'

I spoke more sharply than I'd intended but the boy dint blink. Turning to Memma I explained. 'It's just a nickname some call me. Against my wishes, I might add. I am not a queen and we have no queens hereabouts.'

'Then who'st rules this land?'

The hunter answered. 'We rule ourselves if there's any ruling to be done. Mostly there's just surviving, with little time left over for ordering others about.'

I changed the subject. 'A balloon? What is that?'

Memma made a shape with her hands in the air like an egg on its side.

'Like an egg?' I said.

'Aye! Full o' gas lighter than air.'

'What makes your bath – I mean, basket – fly? And how'd you come to crash?' Dog-boy asked.

'The silk envelope is inflated with gas and rises, lifting mine basket through the air and above the clouds. The accident occurred when an air current caused us to rise too high, the silks froze, becoming heavy with ice, and then I began an uncontrolled descent. I shed all the weight I could by throwing precious cargo o'er, but still 'twas a hard landing.'

'Looked like a crash to me,' Dog-boy insisted.

Memma pursed her lips but did not argue.

'What usually happens when the silk becomes icy?' the hunter asked.

'I hath nev'r encountered such an uprising air current. 'Tis uncharted. A meteorologist hast nev'r been this far into the lower latitudes in modern times.'

'What's above the clouds, madame?' Dog-boy asked. 'I mean, we saw it once but not for long,' he added, looking at me.

'Above the clouds is sky, young sir. And yond thither are the heavens.'

Dog-boy opened his mouth with another question but Memma interrupted. 'Enough. Anon, I must beginneth repairs. If thou pleas't, sir, fetch mine silks inside.'

'I think she wants you to get the fabrics for her,' I told the hunter.

For the rest of the evening and into the night Memma worked on repairing the holes and tears in the enormous volume of silk she called her balloon. She burrowed in her pockets, coming up with a needle and thread, and with tiny stitches, she patched and mended by the light of the fire, nipping off the thread with her sharp teeth, occasionally stopping to blow on her fingers to warm them.

When I stirred at first light, Memma was asleep, wrapped in her silks. Dog-boy lay near the hearth curled up with Poke, and the hunter had only recently risen, judging from the warmth in the blanket he'd left behind. I got to my feet quietly and went outside. Memma's flying craft sat where Poke had pulled it, covered now in a sifting of snow. I brushed it off gently, leaning inside for a look. The inner edges of the basket were lined with instruments, some with softly blinking blue lights, a few giving readings in numbers and letters, but none that I could make sense of. There were lockers built into the sides, latched and not locked and though I were curious, I were not rude enough to poke through them. A small box sat in the bottom of the craft with a number of lids screwed shut and arrows and warnings in red.

'That must be the machine that makes the lifting gas.'

I put my hand to my heart in fright. 'Don't sneak up on a person like that, Dog-boy,' I said gruffly.

'Weren't sneaking, miss. Just my natural light step, I suppose.'

'What do you mean *lifting gas*?'

'She said her balloon is filled with a gas lighter than air. That's not something you can just snatch up, it's got to be made out of the 'lements.'

'*Elements*,' said the hunter, approaching from the forest with two dead rabbits hanging from his belt.

'Hydrogen, I'm guessing,' Dog-boy said.

'Most likely,' said the hunter. 'Though it's just as likely to blow your head off as send you through the clouds.'

'That machine probably splits water into oxygen and hydrogen.'

The hunter nodded. 'But what does she use as a catalyst?'

'Could be zinc, or copper. Could be some other we never heard of.'

I was at a loss. 'How'd you both know about the elements and gases, then?'

The hunter raised his eyebrows at me. 'Common enough knowledge, Snow.'

I frowned in confusion.

Dog-boy pointed to the red arrow. 'What does this say?'

'Danger,' I said, able to read well enough.

'That's all you need to know, miss,' Dog-boy said, turning to follow the hunter into the hut with a superior air.

I were annoyed but just then Memma appeared in the doorway and rushed, limping, toward her craft.

She flicked open the catches on the lockers and searched through them one at a time, then went back to look in each again. She scanned the floor of the basket and pushed aside the neatly rolled lines and straps to look beneath them.

'What's wrong, madame?' I asked her.

'Whither is't? I hath been out of mine own mind, peradventure 'twas altitude sickness. I did dream I threw it overboard, but t'wasn't a dream! What ev'r possess'd me? We must returneth and findeth. T'otherwise I'll be'est maroon'd on this backwards island always.'

'Oy, easy, madame. No need to go around casting shade on places you don't rightly know and people who were kind enough to run to your assistance yesterday,' Dog-boy objected, having understood enough to take offence.

'Calm down, everyone,' I said. 'And you shush,' I said particular-liken to Dog-boy. 'Memma, what have you lost? Perhaps we can find a replacement, or make you a new one.'

The bird-woman scientist-aeronaut turned her pale blue eyes on me mournfully. 'All is lost unless we findeth the catalyst.'

At the mention of a catalyst the hunter and Dog-boy looked at each other and nodded in satisfaction.

A risky search

By the morning proper we were retracing our steps, back to the crash site. Poke pulled the flying craft again, tail wagging. This time Memma sat at the bow, peering out keenly, scanning the ground ahead. She bade us look out for a strongbox, made of metal, containing a powder that Memma, in her confusion and panic, had tossed over the side of the craft in an effort to slow its plunge. She hadn't meant to throw it, but from what I could gather, the lack of oxygen high above the clouds could slow and confuse a person's thinking. The powder, along with plain old water, were added to the machine to create the gas that filled the balloon. It were all simple enough, and nothing to get all high and haughty over one person knowing more'n another. I were annoyed with the hunter and Dog-boy and I'd given the order we were going to look for the box without asken anyone's opinions.

I walked beside the craft as it slid over the snowy ground, Poke pulling like he'd been born for it, tongue hanging out the side of his mouth and ears pointed forward. Little Bear was suspicious of the flying craft and wandered wide, following along in her own way.

I slowly gathered from Memma that she was circumnavigating the whole round earth by flying above the clouds. I got the hang of how to understand her strange speech by not listening to every word, but instead letting her talk wash over me and then getting the gist. She told me that she studied the weather.

'Int any weather here except cold and now even colder,' I told her. 'Except that one time when the clouds broke up for a while.'

'When wast that?' Memma asked.

'Two seasons ago,' I told her. 'Two long nights,' I explained when she looked puzzled.

'Aye! You mean winter.'

'Winter in the old way. But there can't be winter if there int any summer, madame, so sometimes the nights are long and sometimes they are short. That's the only difference.'

'Hmm,' Memma said. 'This is the case all o'er the earth.'

I had many more questions for Memma, someone who had seen the actual world, not just the next mountain or the next island, but everything that can be seen from a perch high in the sky, the whole world.

'I canst see the earth, from on high,' Memma explained. 'Once I'm above the clouds, thither I stayeth, with the stars. Until I descendeth through the clouds again, I canst see what awaits me.'

This was strange to think about. Travelling the world above the clouds without seeing any of what's below.

We reached the crash site and spread out, Memma standing in the basket and pointing us all in different directions. Little Bear and Poke joined the search, seeming to understand we were looking for something, and it dint matter what it was.

We found nothing on the tussock plain upon which Memma had landed and after some hours we regrouped around the basket where Memma waited anxiously.

'Best follow back along the flight path she came down on,' the hunter suggested. 'A heavy box like that is likely to have fallen straight down, crashing through the tops of trees. Sooner we get to it, less likely it'll be buried in fresh snowfalls.'

Memma bobbed down in her basket, consulting her instruments. 'Snow will arrive by tomorrow morning,' she reported.

Dog-boy leaned into the basket. 'You can foretell the weather?'

'Aye! 'Tis my profession, young sir,' said Memma.

Dog-boy raised his eyebrows in a rare show of respect.

'I could've told you it's going to snow, Dog-boy,' the hunter said scornfully. 'Int it always either snowing or about to?'

'In that case, less chatten, more moving,' said Dog-boy.

Poke was harnessed to the balloon-basket once again and Dog-boy held onto the back to slow its descent in parts for now we were heading downhill, toward the forest line and east. I caught the hunter's eye as we set off in this direction.

'Well, I know what you're thinken, Snow. Let's not be alarmed and instead keep an eye out.'

He told me this, what I already knew, because we were walking toward territory that we usually kept clear of. Not because of laws, but out of respect and not a small amount of fear, if I'm honest. It were Stoat's range, the hunter who'd shot an arrow through my chest. By accounts we'd heard he moved in the country we were venturing into now, no longer working for my wicked stepmother, Rain, but still, a person of questionable character that the hunter and I would rather not run across in the dark, or the light for that matter.

Memma again consulted her instruments and calculated her crash trajectory. However, it were one thing to descend over the mountains in a plummeting flying-craft, it were another entirely to go uphill and down over difficult country on foot. The hunter guided us in the general direction, and we spread out to look for the strongbox as much as we could but there were so few of us and so much high country, we might easily walk right past it.

As the light faded and the snow clouds piled up ahead of us, I called a halt to the search, sayen what was obvious, even to Memma. 'We need to find shelter.'

The hunter and I came together to discuss whether we might make it to the caves on the pass above us. Considering the weight Poke was towing, we dint like our chances.

'We could leave the craft, and we could carry her,' I suggested to the hunter.

'Nay! Nay! I canst leave the balloon,' Memma said. 'But . . .' She bent down and undid more catches and revealed more lockers in the bottom of the basket. Turning and pressing a knob she said, 'Stand clear!'

From the base of the basket emerged a pole that lengthened telescopically upwards. We found ourselves standing under a cone-shaped frame as high as the hunter with his arms raised. 'Now, covereth with t' silk,' Memma indicated, waving her arms to show us how. Soon we stood in a tent of fabric, with the balloon basket at the centre. The pole formed the frame and the silks tucked into the snow made a seal against drafts. It was already warm, to my surprise.

'The silk holds heat, naturally, to add lift,' Memma explained.

So with the body heat of four humans, a large bear and a huge dog, we were already feeling cosy.

'Might've been quite a useful trick to show us before the long haul to the hut last night,' grumbled Dog-boy.

After three days of searching and camping in Memma's tent, we were no closer to finding her strongbox.

'Like looking for a pine needle in a pile of pine needles,' Dog-boy said unhelpfully.

Memma wrung her hands as the days passed with no success. We'd backtracked to where her compass told her she'd started her plunge to the ground and we'd crisscrossed our tracks but with fresh snow falling all the time, and no melt likely for months, if ever, I felt it were a lost cause.

Under the silk tent I told Memma we were out of supplies, and needed to return to the chateau and work out another plan. She nodded her reluctant agreement, slumped in the bottom of her basket.

'What about another catalyst for your machine?' asked Dog-boy. 'You're a scientist, aren't you? Can't you make one? There must be something else that will juice it up?'

Memma frowned. 'Thou art very strange. But aye, thither may be'est alternatives.'

'When we get back to the big house we can ask the mister. He's a strange fish, but his head is stuffed full of knowledge,' Dog-boy said. And then, patting Memma's head, 'Don't worry, madame, we'll get you flying away again.'

I glanced at the hunter with raised eyebrows.

Breaking camp we turned toward the chateau. On our way past the crash site the hunter left us, scouting up the mountain.

'Someone else saw her come down,' he said when he rejoined us. 'There were fresh prints. Human,' he added. 'Likely Stoat or one of his men, I'd say.'

'Doubtful they found anything,' I said.

'Except the tracks of a bath that appeared out of nowhere,' Dog-boy said with a lopsided smile. 'That'll be a puzzle.'

'Don't want them being curious,' the hunter said. 'That'll lead to trouble.'

Dog-boy's experiment

We were greeted by a buzzing crowd when the gates of the chateau opened late that same day. Almost everyone had gathered in the bailey to see Poke pull the flying craft safely behind our high walls. Memma looked around in surprise, and shook hands as people came forward to greet her. Dog-boy guided Poke into the great hall, and with many willing hands lifted Memma and the basket over the threshold onto the dry floor. That evening we all ate together at long tables, the fires burning.

Memma sat with her foot on a low stool, fascinated by the children and the animals that gathered with us. Though it were not entirely civilised to eat with goats and dogs and birds and bears, all were welcomed inside on nights such as these. It were my hall and my rules.

Memma had some difficulty, however, making herself understood, and she were asked many questions about where she'd come from, and how she'd arrived. Late in the evening someone pulled in a chalkboard and asked Memma to draw an explanation of her craft. She stood and hopped over to oblige. She started by drawing a huge oblong, as she'd shown me, and drew lines to connect it to the basket that hung underneath. She drew a smaller diagram that showed an opening at the bottom and top of the balloon and arrows to show that gas went in and could be sealed in, causing the balloon to rise, and then vented from the hole in the top in order to descend. A propeller at the stern helped to direct the balloon, though she made it clear that the balloon travelled with the air currents above the clouds and could not go against them.

In answer to a question about the nature of the gas, she wrote a formula on the chalkboard consisting of numbers and letters and lines. It were beyond my understanding but I saw Dog-boy and the mister with their heads together in close discussion.

For the next few days life in the chateau returned to normal. Except that the mister suspended lessons and he and our guest and Dog-boy began spending long hours in the library gathered around the chalkboard. Maps and tables of elements were spread out on the school tables. Memma's ankle improved slowly and she was able to hobble around, observing and contributing to their discussions.

I was forced to take over the children's reading and writing lessons in the kitchen, which caused Cook no end of annoyance as her table was taken over by pencils and dog-eared books.

One day Dog-boy appeared and asked for a supply of bowls and utensils including a rubber tube and mortar and pestle, searching through cupboards and making a mess until Cook chased him out. Dog-boy, juggling what he'd managed to steal, took the main stairs back to the library. After lessons, I followed him up to see what was happening.

A whole table had been taken over with an elaborate experiment. Cork-stoppered glass bottles were suspended over candles connected together by rubber tubes. Another glass jar sat upside down in a tub of water, connected to the other bottles by a tube running under the water. Dog-boy, Memma and the mister huddled together, conversing rapidly. Behind them the experiment that was laid out on the table was represented in a chalked diagram, with the numbers and letters I recognised from Memma's formula. One of the glass jars contained some metal shavings which I were alarmed to see had been ground away from Cook's spoons. While I watched, the metal shavings began to bubble. A few moments later, there was a loud bang and the up-ended bottle in the tub of water was launched toward the ceiling and then smashed on the floor. I took fright and jumped but Dog-boy, Memma and the mister cheered. However this was rapidly followed by a deflation of their spirits as they turned to contemplate the smashed glass on the floor.

'What happened?' I asked.

'The experiment was a success. We made the lifting gas,' the mister answered. 'But also a failure, because our catalyst is too unstable. And we would need all of Cook's spoons – all of the spoons in the land in fact – to make enough catalyst for Memma's fuel cells,' he finished glumly.

This was alarming. 'An explosion any larger than that int happening under my roof,' I told them, glancing at the dent in the ceiling.

'This is the work doth take place in the machine I hath brought with me,' Memma explained. ''Tis advanc'd technology, manufactur'd in a large factory in an even larger city.'

'I'd like to see that,' Dog-boy said.

'Aye. Thou art living in a land time did forget hither in the higher latitudes, young sir.'

'So what will you do now?' I asked them.

Before Memma could answer the hunter appeared in the doorway. 'Snow, you need to come.'

We hurried to the tower and climbed to where we could see outside of the chateau walls.

The hunter said, 'The captain of the watch saw him and closed the gates.'

'Good thinking,' I replied. Because standing outside the walls was Stoat and a straggly group of men. He wore a crossbow across his back and a quiver of arrows on his shoulder, for all I knew containing the exact same one he'd once shot through my chest. He wore leathers and a long coat, all dark in colour. Soon, glancing up, he saw us.

'So there are folks at home,' he said. 'I were knocking loud enough, and no one come to answer. I thought all were welcome through these gates?'

'Not all, not all the time,' I called in response. 'Those who have shot me tryen to kill me are not usually invited to do the same again.'

'Come now, Little Queen,' Stoat laughed mockingly. 'Let's put bygones behind us. I int here to kill you this time. In fact, I got something you might be looking for.'

He reached into a pocket and pulled out an iron box, dark grey, the same colour as Memma's basket.

'Found it over the ridge, thereabouts,' he said, gesturing toward Memma's crash site. 'One of my men took fright,' he explained, 'when he saw a giant bird fall to the ground from above the clouds. Know anything about that?'

Memma had joined us, limping up the stairs and peering down, gripping the top of the wall. She gasped and put her hand to her mouth when she saw what Stoat held.

'Ah!' he said. 'So 'tis what you seek.' And then to me. 'Seems we have some negotiating to do, Little Queen. Open your gates and invite me in to warm my frozen feet at your fire.'

I turned to the hunter and Memma.

'He hast mine strongbox!' she said.

'He'll likely want a price for it we can't pay,' the hunter said.

I agreed. 'He's certainly not going to part with it out of the good of his cold heart.'

'I wilt hath it back, Snow. Mine worketh is of the utmost importance. I shall payeth, whatever the price.'

'As you wish, Memma,' I told her, hoping she did not come to regret her words.

'Lay down your weapons, Stoat,' the hunter called. 'Leave them all there in the snow before we'll open our gates to you. We have children and old people behind these walls. There will be no violence, do you hear me?'

Stoat shrugged his agreement and began to remove his crossbow and quiver, dropping them on the ground. His men threw down an assortment of knives and small firearms.

The hunter ordered the gate opened and Stoat and his men were patted down before being escorted across the bailey to the great hall where they were sat to wait.

A while later, after trying to explain to Memma exactly who we were dealing with, we descended from the wall. I'd even unlaced my coat to show her the scar on my chest that Stoat's arrow had made. But she were determined to recover her box.

We found Stoat and his men sprawled before the fire, boots off, picking over the meal they'd been served, becoming rowdy as they enjoyed our hospitality. Memma and Dog-boy insisted on joining the hunter and I for the negotiations. The mister came as well but hung back in the shadows of the doorway, his cowardice getting the better of his curiosity.

'Ah! So this is the creature that fell from the sky?' Stoat said when he saw Memma.

I began. 'May I introduce Madame Eveline-Madeline-Marie-Adelaide, Official Scientist-Aeronaut of the Restoration.'

Stepping forward, Memma held out her hand. 'You may address me as Madame Memma.'

'May I now?' Stoat taunted, ignoring her offer of a handshake. 'I am not usually in need of such a heavy title, unlike those hereabouts,' he said, with a sneer in my direction. 'Though you may call me Lord Stoat of the East, if you like.'

At this his men guffawed, one of them snorting beer from his nose into his beard.

Memma took all of this in with her wide blue eyes. 'I believeth thee hast found an object yond belongs to me,' she said.

'What'd she say?' Stoat said to his men. And then to Memma, 'We don't talk so fancy around here, missus.'

The hunter stepped in. 'Mind your manners, Stoat. There's no need for jibes and insults.'

Stoat eyed the hunter and turned back to Memma, pulling out the box. 'You mean this?'

Memma's eyes widened and she held out her hand to take it but Stoat pulled it away at the last second. 'Ah, not so fast, lady. What's it worth?'

Memma grew still. 'I hath nothing of value to exchange for what is already mine. 'Tis of nay useth to thee, sir. Please returneth.'

'Show me the flying machine,' Stoat demanded. 'Then we can talk.'

We all of us exchanged glances, instinctively reluctant to reveal Memma's basket and balloon. But it were Memma's to show or not to show and before we could decide what to do, she limped to the back of the hall and pulled the covers aside to reveal where we'd stowed her craft.

Stoat wandered over to examine the balloon silks and basket, leaning in for a better look at the hydrogen elixir engine which sat blinking its red lights as it always did.

'This goes in there?' Stoat surmised, shaking the box and pointing.

Memma nodded tightly in reply.

'And then it flies?'

'That is correct, sir. Anon, may I hath the catalyst, prithee.'

'She talks funny, don't she?' Stoat said, addressing Dog-boy, who was hovering protectively at Memma's elbow. And then, 'Catalyst, you say?'

The hunter winced, as did I. Stoat was wily and cunning and he could smell valuables from as far off as he could smell his prey.

'What exact kind of metal?' he asked.

''Tis not the pretty kind for making jewels and hast no value except for powering the engine of mine own craft. Without it to maketh the gas, the balloon shall not lift and I cannot continueth mine journey.'

Stoat appeared to consider what Memma said. 'You're wrong about it not being valuable, missus. Everything of rarity has a value around here.'

'It doesn't belong to you,' I told him.

'Finders are keepers, Little Queen,' he told me flatly.

'I hath nothing of value to exchange,' Memma said again.

'So you said,' Stoat replied, his pointy beard twitching, his wide-set black eyes darting from the balloon to Memma to the box.

We waited, holding our breath. Even Little Bear and Poke, ears perked, sensed the tension.

'Seems to me the craft and the fuel belong together and also seems to me that I'll be taking both.'

'No!' cried Dog-boy, jumping forward. The hunter reached out and grabbed his arm to hold him back.

Memma stepped up and spoke quickly to Stoat. 'If I come with thee, you will return the box to mine own keeping?' Memma said.

'What? Go with them? What are you talking about?' Dog-boy cried, pulling at the hunter's grip.

Memma had become still and quiet, her wide pale eyes resting on Stoat.

'It's up to you where you go, missus. But I'll be taking the flying machine and the catalyst with me.'

'Then I shall cometh as well.'

'No, Memma! You can't!' Dog-boy cried. 'These are bad men. They will not do as they say they will.'

He squirmed to be rid of the hunter but the older man's grasp was firm.

41

Stoat looked sideways at Dog-boy. 'Have we met?'

Dog-boy went limp and shook off the hunter's hand, but his one-eyed gaze hardened.

'It may be of use to you to remember if we have, before this is said and done,' he replied coldly.

Memma was gathering the silks into the basket. 'I am ready,' she told Stoat, one hand resting on the edge of the basket.

It were all happening too fast for me to take in. 'Wait! Memma, you're leaving us? You're going with these men?'

'That is correct, Miss Snow. I am clear in mine own understanding. The expedition must continueth, yond is mine priority. I thank thee for thy help and hospitality.'

'And that's it?' I were dumbfounded. 'After everything?'

'Mine thanks,' Memma repeated to me. And once again to Stoat, 'I am ready for departure anon.'

Within a few minutes, the gates were opened and Stoat and his men were leaving, this time carrying the basket between them, arguing over its weight and awkwardness. Memma limped quietly behind.

Outside, the men placed the basket in the snow. Memma stepped inside before the men began sliding it over the snow in jerks and pulls. Not as smooth and quiet as Poke had done.

We four – Dog-boy, the hunter, the mister and me – stood watching after them in stunned silence.

'How could you just let them take her?' Dog-boy shouted at me and ran toward the kitchen, Poke trotting after him loyally.

'Dog-boy!' I called after him but had no reply. I turned to the hunter. 'What just happened?'

'She's a grown woman, I guess,' he said. 'Makes her own decisions.'

There was no backward look from Memma.

'Close the gate,' I told the watch.

A visit to the tomb

←———《

Since Memma's departure with Stoat and his men, Dog-boy had stood watch on the wall, staring one-eyed through the binocs, scanning the sky for Memma's balloon. He'd almost frozen to death more than once up there but refused to come down, claiming he'd see the balloon ascend, even in the dark, for its silver silks would reflect on the clouds. The longer the wait the more worried he'd become, convinced that Stoat and his men were keeping the aeronaut captive, rather than giving the catalyst back and letting her continue her journey. I'd tried to tell him that Stoat had never promised to give anything back. He'd stolen the balloon and Memma chose to go with them rather than be parted from her craft.

'You could've put up more of a fight for her,' he said to me.

'Maybe I could've, and for that I'm sorry. I'm sorry you lost a friend.'

'She weren't my friend, exactly,' Dog-boy said. 'But I thought we had an understanding. I thought we were going to help her get back up in her balloon. And I thought maybe she might help us lift the clouds.'

'There int any lifting the sky, Dog-boy. Not by magic or science. Only the passing of time.'

'You don't understand, miss,' Dog-boy said sadly. 'I think she knows how to. She dint want to tell us, because she was still gathering her data. But I think she thinks there's a way. It haven something to do with the mountains on this island that long ago blew their tops and cast fire and ash into the sky. But none of that matters if she can't float her balloon. Without the catalyst, there's no hope. Her basket may as well be made of rocks.'

I sighed. 'You understand that she went with Stoat because that were her only choice?'

'Yes, miss, but what kind of a choice is that to make? Who's to say Stoat won't cut her throat and sell the balloon for its novelty?'

I swallowed hard, there being no one who knew more'n me what Stoat would do for the highest price.

That were when a memory was stirred in my mind. Thinking of the fire-mountain Dog-boy mentioned made me remember something from a very long time ago. Something my father told me before he died. I hurried down from the tower and found the hunter. We were going to dig for some buried treasure.

The hunter worked beside me pulling down the sealed entrance stone by stone. He cast glances my way from time to time, to see if I were still determined.

'Keep going,' I told him. 'I'm sure.' We knelt on frozen ground, down the way from the chateau. When the dark entrance was revealed, I bent to light a lamp and held it aloft as we entered.

The tomb ran long and deep, sloping gently away into heavy snowfall. The more dead there were, the more it had been dug out over the years. The oldest bodies were in the entrance, those more recently placed in their shrouds were further and further away down the icy tunnel. Names and next of kin were written on plaques beneath each resting place, the corpses lying stacked on wooden shelves, like books in our library. Our footfalls crunched on the icy floor, the sound dulled and softened in the cavern. The hunter had to duck his head in parts as the ceiling hung low. It made him look like he walked with head bowed. We passed row on row of shelved dead, wrapped and sewn into woollen blankets frozen stiff. Some were placed on boughs of aromatic pine, the tips still green in the lamplight and smelling like the forest above our heads. In places roots reached down toward us, breaking through into empty space. The way opened into branched chambers, so that we had to duck into those to be thorough in our search. The hunter's face was drawn and white.

'Go back,' I told him, seeing how hard he was taking it. He shook his head and stepped past to lead the way.

Finally we'd walked through the years far enough. I held the lantern close to read each name and find the one I wanted. There was my father's first wife, a bony figure wrapped in soft wool dyed a light blue, and close by her was my father, cloaked in a blanket woven from threads shot through with gold and silver. I placed a hand on the wrapped form and closed my eyes a moment to remember him.

Seeing I'd gone too far in the order of burial then, I retraced our steps and, bending low, found a tomb we'd passed by. The plaque showed no name, but the shroud held the body of a woman about my size and frame.

'Snow, I can look for you.'

'No, I'll see for myself.'

The hunter held the lamp and, kneeling, I pulled aside the shroud covering my mother's face. The mother who birthed me and died in the trying.

The hunter let out a long breath. 'You could be twins.'

Frozen all these years, her skin were grey and lips white from frost, but her hair fell loose in glossy lengths, just as mine did. We looked to be the same age.

I gazed at her face but there was nothing to read there. Not who she was or where she'd come from. Not who my ancestors were or why her people hadn't wanted me.

'There int any more to see, Snow. Let's get back to the living,' the hunter said.

'Just a minute,' I told him, sorry for bringing up his bad memories of seeing frozen bodies but needing to look now and then leave the girl to rest in whatever peace she could find.

I pulled the shroud away further, until her hands showed, crossed over her chest. And there I saw a small pouch, held between her fingers. I pulled it carefully from her frozen grasp and replaced her veil.

Catching the hunter's hand I led him back past the rows of dead and out under the clouds once more. Emerging into the light, the hunter turned his face to the clouds and breathed deeply. Loosening the cord at the top of the pouch, I carefully tipped the contents into my palm. They were dull metal coins, heavily tarnished, making the fine engravings hard to make out. On one side was an image of an old man wearing a crown, on the other a mountain missing its peak.

The hunter examined one of the coins. 'Who's this?'

47

'They used to depict kings and queens on coins in the old days,' I said, turning it over and looking closely at the mountain.

'A volcano,' said the hunter.

I nodded in agreement. 'But what of the metal?'

'Not silver,' he said then, tapping it against his teeth. 'Not nickel neither, or copper.'

The hunter and I found Dog-boy up on the wall and I tipped the strange heavy coins into the palm of his hand.

'What are—? Hell's teeth!' he swore, pressing one of the coins between his thumb and first finger. He felt the metal and then squinted at the fire-mountain with his good eye. 'Where'd you get this?' Without waiting for an answer, he leapt to his feet. 'We gotta show the mister!'

And he was off and racing along the wall, down the steps and across the bailey, scattering a flock of chickens in his path. Poke, awoken suddenly from sleep, took off after the boy, causing the chickens to squawk and fly up into the goat shed eaves.

'I told him, no scaring the chickens,' I sighed.

The hunter and I followed. By the time we arrived in the library, Dog-boy and the mister were hard at work replicating the experiment they'd done with Memma. Dog-boy was holding a file and one of my mother's coins over a small dish when the hunter stopped him.

'Just a minute, boy. You need to mind what you're doing. Have you not had cause to wonder where those strange coins have come from? The ones you're about to shave into filings?'

Dog-boy looked up, letting the coin and file fall to the table, appalled. 'Where they from, Miss Snow?'

I were embarrassed somewhat. 'Leave the boy alone,' I told the hunter. 'I give them freely to the cause, Dog-boy. They have been held by my mother in her grave these long years. Helping no one there. So if they are the catalyst we seek, then we should find that out.'

'Are you sure, miss?' Dog-boy said. 'I'm sorry I dint ask permission. This process will damage the coin, though I need only a small shaving.'

'You have my permission,' I told him. 'Go ahead.'

Carefully now, taking only the barest shaving, Dog-boy and the mister proceeded with the experiment. It did not take long. As before, bubbles formed and were carried along the rubber tubes into the upturned glass jar. But this time, though I brought my hand up to shield my eyes, there was no explosion, instead the jar lifted gently, hovering lightly above the water. We stared at it, the hovering glass defying the natural laws of gravity.

'It may remain there for some time,' the mister said quietly. 'The power of the catalyst is considerable, even in such a small sample.'

Dog-boy and the mister were elated. They clasped hands and jumped up and down, congratulating each other before Dog-boy threw himself at me, gripping me in a tight hug and causing Poke to bark excitedly.

I returned Dog-boy's embrace. 'Well done,' I told him.

'Thank you, miss.'

'Now what?' said the hunter.

'We rescue Memma,' Dog-boy said with certainty. 'We leave right away.'

Chasing Stoat

It weren't quite that simple. There were preparations to be made and supplies to gather for what could be a long walk. Dog-boy was properly kitted out with good clothing against the cold this time, and given his share of the food to carry. Even Poke was burdened with saddlebags. We gathered in the bailey so early that our warm breath froze and fell to the ground as powdered ice. Little Bear, sensing another trip beyond the chateau walls, was waiting for us outside the gate.

'Still no idea how she does that,' the hunter said.

I said nothing, giving Little Bear the scratch around her ears she liked so much. Truth was that I dint know either how Little Bear knew when we were on the move. She just did.

Over the evening meal the day before – it were as much as we could do to hold Dog-boy back from racing out through the gates the second his experiment was confirmed – we decided it were likely that Stoat was headed for the city. Letting Memma continue on her mission would not profit him. Letting her continue it from the middle of a city with a paying audience to watch probably would. Our plan was to ambush Stoat and his men and steal Memma back. With the coin catalyst, she could continue on her expedition and be free of any obligation to

Stoat. But to do all that we had to catch Stoat and disarm him.

That part of the plan made me nervous. We were outnumbered and outmuscled. Stoat's cunning was lethal, as I had learned the hard way. The hunter was likewise wary but Dog-boy had a headful of steam and took off down the mountain like his pants were on fire.

It was a fire that were soon put out by the storm that rolled onto us and kept us pinned down in an old shed a day's walk down the mountain. The black clouds pressed low and the wind howled around the stone walls. The iron on the roof rattled and flapped where storms past had worked nails loose and not been repaired. We shared the space with a few straggly sheep and a billy goat that smelled like ripened cheese.

Dog-boy fretted, making Poke whine, even above the noise outside. Poke's whining made the hunter irritable and the sheep shifty. Little Bear went outside and dug herself a quiet snow cave, but I were stuck with the company inside.

'Dog-boy, stop your pacing and sit still a while,' I told him. 'If you're going to live in the mountains you need to learn when it's time to move fast and when to lie low and save energy. I once waited out a week-long storm in a pitch-dark hut with only Little Bear for company. She was only a baby then but she already knew how to wait.'

'Never been good at waiting, miss.'

I sighed. 'Being still takes as much effort as moving, more even. If you won't do it for me, do it for Poke,' I said. 'Look, you're making him crazy and the sheep are going to die of fright.'

Dog-boy finally dropped to his knees by the fire we'd made in an old feed bin. 'Tell me a story, miss. Maybe then I can be quiet and listen.'

So I told him the story of being shut in the west tower by my stepmother for eight years and how she wanted to get rid of me before I were old enough to claim the chateau as my own as my father had wanted.

'So she told the hunter to take me into the forest and gut me like a goat.'

The hunter shifted in discomfort where he lay beside me pretending to sleep. It were not his favourite part of the story.

I went on. 'But he dint kill me, obviously, because we made a deal.'

'What was it?' Dog-boy said.

'I told him I'd marry him when I were grown and it were an offer too good to refuse.'

The hunter snorted in disagreement.

'For my part I were deadly serious but in truth the hunter never had the heart to kill me,' I said. 'He planned to let me go so long as I were never to show my face to my stepmother again. But while we were discussing terms, we were attacked by a she-bear. She came out of nowhere and had me pinned in the snow, just about to gnaw through my ribs, when the hunter drew his weapon and shot her through the heart. It were sad enough to kill a bear but worse to discover a few moments later that she'd been protecting her cub.

'That's how I got Little Bear. In spite of me killen her mother she saved me that night and all the nights to come after. But those are longer stories and I'll tell them another time.'

Dog-boy had become still and quiet.

'Stoat caused the loss of my eye,' he said quietly.

My hand went to my mouth in shock and the hunter sat up in his blankets.

'I told you a lie, before, miss, about my mother finding me spooky. There were a fire in the inn where she worked serving beer. I slept on a shelf under the bar while she poured, just a wee boy. There was an argument one night, there always were, but this time it came to violence and in the chaos a lamp fell, spilling fuel, and the curtains caught alight. In a matter of a few breaths the whole place was ablaze. My mother fell to the floor from breathing in the smoke, trying to get close enough to throw water on the curtains. Men trampled over her where she lay to get themselves to safety. The shelf I lay on collapsed, burning me. Lucky for me one of the maids fished me out of the debris and threw me into the snow. The burns were soothed by the cold but I still lost my eye, and my mother.

'While I lay in the snow, I saw Stoat and his men going into the night, singed and coughing but still laughing.

'After that I were on my own on the city streets until Poke found me. The two of us looked out for each other. I wouldn't have made it without him. Just like you and Little Bear, miss. And I were there the day you woke up from the dead. In the town square. I saw the birds leave the chapel and open the sky. Sometime after that, when the new cold settled in, it were harder and harder to the live off the scraps of others. People started keeping those scraps for themselves. So we decided to come and find you, miss.'

Dog-boy finished his story with a sigh and closed his one eye to sleep.

The hunter and I stared into the flames until the worst of the cold passed and we could lie down as well.

Fox's city

When the storm passed over, we dug our way out and found the road down the mountain. The snowfalls were thigh-deep, waist-deep on Dog-boy. Little Bear broke a path for us and we waded after her. It were slow and cold going and no way to tell if we were on Memma's trail or not.

If we'd been halted by the storm, then so had Stoat, I told Dog-boy, so we just had to keep pushing and we'd come across him sooner or later.

Later the next evening we approached the top of a hill. Keeping low, we peered over and saw that we'd caught up to the gang of thieves. They were camped for the night, a large fire set, and Stoat's men gathered close around. The basket lay to one side with the silks bundled inside. We couldn't see well but assumed that Memma lay under them. She did not offer the basket's tent structure to her captors, instead letting them sleep outside.

It were a cold night in the open for us as well, and with no fire. We kept each other and our animals close for warmth. Dog-boy were all for racing down the hill and plunging into their midst, with nothing but his small fists swinging, but the hunter told him no blasted way. Neither would he agree to Dog-boy's suggestion that he shoot Stoat's men one by one from the cover of the high hill.

'I'm not killen men in cold blood, boy,' he said. 'No matter what their crimes.'

As we watched, Stoat ordered the basket pulled in close to the fire and set a watch over Memma and the flying craft. So there was not going to be any sneaking into the camp and sliding her away quietly.

'So what do we do?' Dog-boy cried.

'We watch and wait,' I told him.

'I'm not good at waiting,' he said. 'I already told you that.'

But even so, he curled up between Poke's legs and closed his eye to sleep.

The hunter and I took turns keeping watch. Stoat rose early next morning and kicked his men awake one by one. Soon after, they were on their way again. I shook the hunter and Poke licked Dog-boy's face to wake him up.

They turned Memma out of her basket to walk and, after an argument among the men about whose turn it was to carry the bulky craft, they set off again in the direction of the city.

We rose from our cold, cramped camp and hurried after them, keeping a safe distance. To my relief, Stoat pushed on for the city that day, not keen on camping out again, no doubt, and by early evening we were on the final approach to Fox's new city, moved back from the sea in the years since my funeral.

Many of the larger houses had been taken apart stone by stone and rebuilt in exact replicas of their originals. Those people with fewer resources had built their new dwellings from the scraps left behind, dragging them along the new road on wagons and carts, their homes filling in the spaces between grander buildings. They looked like wonky shanties, resting against walls and roofed with a mixture of pine thatch and mud. Since the new cold had settled in, some had even built shelters out of ice and snow.

Why not? Nothing to pay and enough ice to build a castle if that was your fancy. And if one day it melts on your head you'll be so glad of the warmth that did it, you'll forget all about your house disappearing into a puddle.

We left Little Bear outside the city, sitting on her backside watching us go. She had no business with cities, and soon turned and made for the treeline to wait. So the three of us and Poke followed Stoat and his men and Memma and her craft into the city, keeping our distance. Stoat had thrown a canvas over the basket to disguise its strangeness, and no one gave him a second look as he passed along the streets. We tracked him to an inn and watched while he stowed Memma's balloon in the stable next door and set two men to guard it. He dragged Memma inside with him, in spite of her digging in her heels. With her long white hair and silver flying suit, she caught some stares on the street before Stoat pulled her inside and closed the door.

'We can find ourselves warm beds too,' I said. 'He int going anywhere now. We'll know soon enough what he intends and then we can plan what to do.'

Dog-boy shifted restlessly, his one good eye darting around.

'You okay, boy?' the hunter asked him.

'Dint realise how I've got used to the quiet behind the walls in your big mountain *chat-oh*,' he replied.

Poke too, was on alert; the fur on his neck was raised and he stuck close to Dog-boy's heels.

'You're safe enough with us,' the hunter told him. 'And you'll not be sleeping rough tonight.'

In the days following, the hunter shadowed Stoat as he moved around the city while Dog-boy, Poke and I kept watch on the inn. Memma did not appear on the street again and the men watching the stable did not waver in their guard duty, relieving each other every four hours, night and day. The hunter reported that Stoat had been to see Mayor Fox, visited several printing houses and spent half a day with a carpenter.

'What's he up to?' I wondered.

'He's planning to put on a show,' Dog-boy said.

And sure enough, that evening we started seeing posters on walls across the city. It were a depiction of Memma's balloon, a little vague on details, as if the artist were having trouble imagining such a thing, but bright on colours and flourishes. There would be a flying show, in two days' time. In the town square. Memma's full name and title, spelling a little wonky, were splashed across the poster along with the appointed day and time, weather permitting. It reminded me of the first time I'd come to the city and being surprised enough to see tall buildings and paved streets but then I'd seen my face on cups and plates and posters and bunting everywhere I looked. My stepmother had been searching for me and the pictures of me and my bear had taken hold of people's imaginations. Now it were Memma's turn to be the latest sensation.

There was a charge for entry into the square which Dog-boy scoffed at. 'Can't make me pay to watch what it'll be plain to see by climbing to any nearby rooftop.'

I dreaded to think what Memma was making of her scientific endeavours being turned into a spectacle for Stoat's profit.

'She's probably planning her escape,' Dog-boy said as we sat over the remains of our dinner the night before the flying display was scheduled. 'Once she's aloft, she'll take her leave.'

'Not if Stoat holds onto her strongbox,' I pointed out. 'Which he definitely will. She cannot risk leaving without it. If she were to crash again, she'd be marooned just as well, if not in worse circumstances.'

'Then we have to get her a message,' Dog-boy said. 'That we have a new supply of catalyst.'

'How do we do that?' the hunter said. 'She's under guard day and night. And I've already said, there's to be no killen, just rescue.'

'No killen needed,' Dog-boy replied. 'The main streets and fancy buildings might not be part of my city but the alleys and drains and back doors are all mine. We'll find a way,' he said, scratching his dog's ears. 'Won't we, Poke? But we'll need some cash,' he said, holding out his open palm to me.

I gave him two copper coins from our small supply as well as one of the fire-mountain coins to show Memma. Dog-boy buttoned them carefully into his trousers pocket. I hoped it were the one pocket in his outfit not full of holes.

That evening Dog-boy let himself out the back door of our inn and took off like a damp shadow with his dog. I paced and the hunter fidgeted as the hours passed.

'He int exactly anonymous, is my thinking,' I said to the hunter. 'If you've seen him once you're likely to remember a small boy with an eye patch and a dog the size of a bear.' I hoped he would not risk being seen by Stoat or any of his men.

'Smart as a rat, that boy,' the hunter said. 'We needn't worry.'

Still we did. It were an eternity before we heard the latch lift on the back door and it opened to Dog-boy, wearing a dark red skirt and trudging muddy prints across the floor. Poke went straight to the fire and lay on his side to warm himself.

'There's good news and not that good,' Dog-boy said as he warmed his backside. 'Good news is I found Memma and spoke to her. The bad I'll get to when you give me a chance to catch my breath.'

Impatient as we were, we let Dog-boy keep us in suspense. I perched on a chair and the hunter sat pretending like he didn't care one way or the other.

After leaving us, Dog-boy said, he threaded his way through the alleys of the city. Alleys where rubbish was stacked and workers make their way between kitchens and laundries and workrooms and storerooms and bakeries and butchers and animal yards and gardens. All the places where the work is done, where everyone has a different specialty. This is the wonder of a city. But Dog-boy dint have an eye for wonder, he was on a mission. Making his way to the back of Stoat's inn, he set himself in a dark corner against a wall, pulling Poke in beside him, and began a watch. He couldn't have said what he was looking for, but he'd know it when he saw it. 'For once I sat still, miss, you'd never have believed it.'

Stoat's man huddled under the dripping porch outside the kitchen, ignoring the cook coming out to smoke a pipe, wiping her hands on her apron and sitting heavily on an upturned pot. There was the dishboy, scraping plates onto the paving for a herd of cats gathered waiting. Dog-boy would've been shooing those cats away to get a mouthful of scrapings himself in the old days but now his stomach was full and he shushed Poke for growling at the cats. It were starting to rain lightly which made the dark night even darker, but still Dog-boy noticed a small person, a girl, pushing a cart over the muddy paving, hood drawn up and fingers gloved. The cart was stacked with clean laundry that the girl was struggling to keep the rain from splashing by holding up an umbrella. Dog-boy rushed to help.

The girl waved him aside. 'I don't have any food or coin for tips,' she told him. 'So don't waste your efforts.'

'Just the opposite,' Dog-boy said. 'Let me explain.'

The girl pushed back her hood and looked at Dog-boy frankly. She had tired circles under her eyes and cheeks rosy from the cold.

'What happened to your eye?' she asked, peering through the gloom.

'My eyeball fell in a pond and a fish ate it,' Dog-boy said.

'Well, if you're going to be rude—' the girl said, pushing past.

'Pretty rude to ask a one-eyed person where their other eye is, don't you think?'

She paused. 'I suppose. Sorry.'

'What's your name?'

'People call me Rose Red. On account of my hair,' she said, pushing back her hood to show her bright red hair. She dint seem pleased about it.

'Rose Red, s'nice to meet you. People call me Dog-boy. Can I borrow your cart and make your delivery for you? See, my friend is held prisoner in this inn and I need to get a message to her.'

Rose Red gasped and put a gloved hand to her mouth. 'Prisoner! Can't you call the watch?'

Dog-boy shook his head impatiently. 'No need for all the fuss. But I do have a desperate need to get past that guard,' he said, nodding toward Stoat's man who stood dark and foreboding by the back door. 'If you let me make your delivery, I'll pay you. And look, you can go and wait with my dog. We got a cosy dry spot over there.'

The girl peered through the darkness to where Poke raised his head obligingly. Her eyes went wide with fear.

'He's big but he's friendly,' Dog-boy said. He'll keep you company while I'm gone.'

'And how long will that be?'

'A minute or two at most, and then, look,' Dog-boy rummaged in his pocket and pulled out one of the copper coins I'd given him.

Rose Red raised an eyebrow. 'Ifen you got another one of those, then we got a deal.'

Dog-boy tipped his head on the side and dropped his shoulders in a show of defeat. 'You driving a hard bargain with a desperate man, girl?'

Rose Red scoffed and folded her arms across her chest.

'Most likely at you suggesting you're a man,' the hunter said, interrupting. Dog-boy ignored him and continued his story.

'If you let me borrow your hood and gloves you got a deal, Rose Red. And your skirt for good measure,' he said, dropping a second coin into her palm.

Rose Red, happy with her bargain, stepped out of the skirt she wore over pants and handed it to Dog-boy, who gave her a shove toward Poke. 'Mind your manners, Poke,' he told the dog. 'Look after Miss Rose.'

Poke smiled and licked the girl's bare hand.

Dog-boy, quickly donning the hood and gloves and pulling Rose's skirt over his trousers, grasped the cart and umbrella and approached the kitchen door. He was ready to make his case for entry but Stoat's man proved to be more gentleman than Dog-boy had given him credit for.

'Here, miss. Lemme lend a hand,' he said, helping lift the cart through the door.

Leaving it at the bottom of the stairs, Dog-boy knocked on each door along the hallway, calling out, 'Fresh linen, sir? Fresh linen, madam?'

As each door opened he kept his head bowed and the hood pulled low over his eye-patch, but no one gave him a second glance. He was all the way at the end of the hall when he had the reply he was looking for. 'Nay, thank thee.'

'Memma!' Dog-boy shout-whispered through the door. ''Tis me! Open up.'

The door opened slowly, Memma's bright eyes appearing in the gap. 'Young sir!'

'Lemme in, madame. I have to speak with you.'

Glancing down the hall, Memma opened the door wider and Dog-boy slipped through.

'This is very dangerous, young sir. Far more than I thought when I undertook to stayeth with mine balloon. Why hath thee followed me hither?'

'We think we've found a new supply of catalyst, madame. You can free yourself of Stoat, if it works.'

Dog-boy explained quickly the source of the coins, and described his successful experiment proudly. Memma asked to see them.

Dog-boy dug in his pocket, pulling out a plain copper. 'Oh

wait,' he said, slapping his forehead. 'I think I gave it to a friend by mistake, but she's just outside. I can show you soon. But believe me, it worked and it will likely fuel your machine.'

'Nay. Go now, young sir. This is mine own dilemma. I cannot involve thee in further danger. Do not concern thyself further with my welfare.'

And with this, she gently pushed Dog-boy out the door.

'But, madame, listen to me. I am certain it will work. When you lift off in your balloon tomorrow, be confident you can float away. Fly back to the chateau and we can make you more catalyst.'

'Even if it be true, I cannot taketh coins from Snow. The lady hath done enough with little to giveth already. I made my bargain with Stoat. At the hour he hath made his money on the morrow, he shall give me the strongbox. I don't needeth thy help, boy. Fare thee well.'

And with this she shut the door firmly.

Dog-boy cursed his careless giving of the fire-mountain coin to Rose Red. He raced back down the hall, collected the cart and rushed into the cold, dark night.

Crossing the paving he found his loyal dog waiting for him, and the girl nowhere to be seen.

'Cripes and custard,' he said, kicking himself. 'I been living inside too long, Poke. I've lost all my wits. Miss Snow's gonna kill me for losing her coin. And Memma won't budge. What do we do now?'

The hunter leaned forward, elbows on his knees. 'Seems to me that's all bad news, boy. You lost a fire-mountain coin and Memma prefers her captors.'

'I'll find the girl and get the coin back. It were an honest mistake made in the dark,' Dog-boy said. 'Sorry, Miss Snow,' he said to me.

'Turns out it weren't the holes in your pockets I should have been worried about,' I told him. 'I thought you had the sharpest eye on the watch? Never mind. Nothing we can do now except get to bed. Stoat's circus starts in a few short hours. We'll stay out of sight and see then what the day brings.'

Dog-boy sat heavily in front of the fire, hanging his head. The hunter patted him on the shoulder as we went up to our bed.

The rain had eased by daylight but been replaced by a gusty breeze. The hunter and I pulled up our hoods and made our way through the crowds that were already gathering in the square. Climbing on some scaffolding leaning against a fine building opposite the main council, we settled to watch and wait. Dog-boy and Poke were already gone when we'd woken.

'He'll catch us up,' the hunter said. 'No one knows the city better'en a street rat.'

From our perch we took in the scene. As the crowd queued, paying for entry one by one, they brought with them an air of sceptical anticipation. They slowly grew in number, standing around the stage Stoat had arranged to be constructed in the middle of the square. On it sat Memma's basket, under heavy guard by black-clad men. The balloon silks lay in a bundle with a mess of straps and ropes wrapped around them. The square had been decorated with colourful flags and streamers, and food carts began to appear at the edges of the crowd. The smell of sweets and savouries filled the air, making my stomach rumble. The mood began to turn from sceptical to light, the people starting to enjoy the festivities, even if they had low expectations of a flying spectacle. The wind was strong enough to lift snow from the paving and blow hats and scarves from heads, but the rain held off.

The hunter nudged me. 'Here she comes.'

The council doors were slowly swinging open, the same ones I'd walked through when I came back to life at my funeral. Today there was no choir of birds, just the street pigeons, intent on their waddling search for edible specks.

Memma emerged, flanked by Stoat and a herald holding a brass horn in one hand. The scientist-aeronaut wore her flying suit, as well as her cap and goggles. She appeared to sniff the air like a mouse and I could see her sharp eyes taking in the crowd and her basket where it sat heavily on the stage.

Stoat signalled to the herald who played a short fanfare on his horn. When the last notes had died away, a hush fell over the crowd and Stoat cleared his throat.

'Welcome one and all,' he began gruffly. 'May I introduce Madame Eveline-Madeline-Marie-Adelaide, Official Aeronaut of the Restoration.'

'The what?' someone called out and was answered with laughs.

Stoat frowned. 'We are about to witness a marvel! Madame will today demonstrate her flying machine. A balloon!' he shouted.

He were not a natural showman, and the crowd shifted restlessly, disliking being shouted at. I glanced at the hunter, unimpressed.

Stoat, clearing his throat, dug in his pocket and read from a scrap of paper, trying to drum up enthusiasm. 'After some brief preparations, the balloon will lift off, floating free of the earth, in a wondrous display of flying. Please give madame a round of applause.'

With this there was some scattered obedient clapping but the air of scepticism had returned.

As the morning passed, we watched as Memma directed Stoat's men with sharp orders in her strange tongue that they struggled to understand. As a result, progress was slow and we could see Stoat becoming impatient, pacing up and down at the top of the council steps, his herald leaning against a column, yawning.

The crowd had initially surged forward when Memma appeared, but now they drifted, some sitting on the cold ground, the children running in circles. Gradually Memma succeeded in getting Stoat's men to anchor the basket with ropes tethered to the ground. This took some doing as all the ropes needed to be untangled first. Next she threw the balloon silks across the paved square and started arranging more straps and flaps. The size of the silks laid out that way pushed the crowd back into the corners of the square, with Stoat's men chasing children off the fabric.

Finally, at a signal from Memma, Stoat descended the council stairs and mounted the stage. Again, the sleepy herald played a fanfare, this time summoning some energy and playing at some length until Stoat turned an icy glare his way and he faltered to a stop.

'In this box I hold the magical elixir that powers the flying craft,' Stoat told the crowd, holding the box above his head. Memma looked at her strongbox, the longing in her hard stare visible even from our distance. She climbed into her basket and held out her hands for the box. Stoat handed it over and

Memma crouched in the bottom to replenish the machine. He signalled to Memma that she should begin the demonstration. The crowd stood on tiptoe trying to see.

What followed this brief action was more waiting as the silks were slowly filled with gas. For a long time it seemed that it were only the gusty wind stirring and lifting the balloon silk. Tired children went to lie on their bored mothers' laps. The food vendors, sold out of product, leaned against their carts and gossiped.

Finally, the balloon started to take shape. The gas lifted the fabric from the icy paving, gently floating in the breeze. At first it looked like a droopy flag with no wind to stir it but gradually it took on an oval shape and began lifting from the ground on its own.

At last, well into the day, my backside feeling cold and numb from sitting, the silks were filled with gas and now hovered over the basket, taking up almost all of the sky above the square, and throwing a cold shadow across half of the crowd. Now people were on their feet and more customers were queuing at the gate, handing over their admission coin. Stoat leaned against a column at the top of the council steps, smiling smugly. Soon the square was packed with folk standing elbow-to-elbow, gazing up at the balloon in wonder.

It were a stunning sight to see. The grey silks shimmered and shone, buffeted by the wind. Memma was busy in the basket, tightening lines and checking the sandbags that hung over all sides of the basket. When the wind rose, we could see her peering up at the balloon, and though it were too far to see her expression, concern was written clearly in her stance.

Once again Stoat ordered a fanfare, and this time did not

interrupt as the horn-player built to a crescendo. Judging the moment, Memma hurried to each side of the basket in turn and released sand from her weighted bags. Each emptied into a swirling pile on the stage, blown up by the wind and flicking into the eyes of those gathered close. The basket began to stir. Memma released the next sandbag and another and the basket rose smoothly, still tethered by long rope lines. As the balloon rose to the height of the houses in the square, Memma began to loosen the ties she'd had Stoat's men fix one by one. She rose higher, and then higher than the council roof. Now the whole city, those paying spectators in the square as well as those going about their everyday business, turned toward the astounding sight. The balloon rose steadily and we could see Memma, even smaller now, high above us, place her hand on the tiller of her balloon, turning the spinning propeller in the air and directing the basket downwind.

However, there was an extra line that she had not seen, attached to the underneath of the basket. It was a line Stoat had secretly fixed. And the one that would prevent her continuing on her expedition.

As she released her final sand bag the last rope drew taut and the balloon jerked to a stop. Memma was thrown forward in the basket heavily. For a few moments we could not see her but then there she was, peering over the edge of the basket to see which line was caught. It did not take her long, a breath or two, to see what Stoat had done. How he had tricked her. And then she sank out of sight again.

The audience did not seem to notice that this was not part of the show. They continued to clap and cheer and hoist their children to their shoulders for a better look.

Stoat gave another signal to his men and they pulled open a trapdoor in the top of the stage. Underneath two men began to work a handle on an enormous reel, slowly spooling the tether and bringing Memma and her balloon back to earth.

All in all it were a horrifying spectacle, made all the worse by the crowd being none the wiser of the deception. My hand went to my mouth and the other gripped the hunter's arm.

'We've got to help her,' I said softly through my shock.

'Not two of us against all of them we can't,' the hunter said. 'Besides, we got another problem.'

He nodded to a skirmish below us in the crowd. I instantly recognised the lean figure of Dog-boy forcing his way through the packed square toward Memma, Poke following in his wake. He was shouting curses and abuse aimed at Stoat. I jumped to my feet and climbed down off the scaffolding, closely followed by the hunter. Trying to be polite, we pushed though the gathering with excuse me's and pardons, getting along a little quicker than Dog-boy with his shouting and shoving. We reached him just before he got close enough to launch himself at the stage, holding him firmly between us and walking him back, heads down, hoods up.

By the time we reached a quiet backstreet, he'd gone limp between us, dragging his feet with his head hanging.

'Don't take it so hard, boy,' the hunter said as we sat him on a step and Poke got close enough to lick the tears from his friend's face. 'We gotta bide our time and plan what to do next.'

We sat there, waiting for Dog-boy to gather himself.

The crowd began to disperse. The spectacle had taken all day and now the air was growing cold as the evening crept in. It were time for people to get home to stoke their fires and cook their evening meals. The mood was high in those who passed us by, children chattering and asking questions about flying their parents had no answers for, none of them knowing any better that Memma were never meant to be tied to the ground.

While we waited for dark to creep in a little more before we walked back to our inn, Poke jumped up and ran toward a girl who was approaching cautiously out of the gloom further down the alley.

'Poke knows you,' I told her as she approached.

Dog-boy looked up and, seeing her, jumped to his feet, fists clenched. 'I been looking for you all day, you cheat.'

'Well, I been looking for you all day as well,' the girl said defensively, lifting her chin. 'Soas to give you back your coin,' she continued. 'I will admit that I were tempted to hold onto it, but I heard you been asken after me all day and I see it's valuable to you so I'm glad to swap it for the copper you intended to pay me.'

'Pork pies, Rose Red!' Dog-boy said. 'More like you tried to trade it and no sellers would take it from you, seeing as it's clearly not city coin.'

I took it the girl was the one who'd lent Dog-boy her laundry cart. She looked about the same age as him, a little taller, wearing trousers under a skirt and a hood that half-covered her bright red hair.

'I could have passed it off anytime I wanted,' Rose Red said.

'I doubt it. Just a girl like you—'

'*Just a girl!* Who do you think you are, *just a boy*?'

'I'm Snow,' I said, standing up and getting between the two. 'And this is the hunter.'

The girl politely shook my hand. Digging in her skirt pocket she held out the fire-mountain coin Dog-boy had given her accidentally.

'This is yours, miss. And I know who you are already,' she told me. 'You're the Little Queen who came back to life and lifted the clouds.'

I sighed. 'Not exactly. Would you like to eat with us tonight, Rose Red? Poke is asken,' I said, nodding to the dog who had gone back to licking her hand.

Over our meal, Rose Red told us she'd been raised by her grandmother in the old city, and came along with everyone else when Fox moved it inland, away from the rising waves. Up-ended into the new city, they struggled. They'd had to leave their cottage which had kept them warm and where her grandmother raised chickens and sold chicks and eggs at the market, making just enough for them to get by. Boxed in at the city's new housing where people lived on top of one another, they couldn't keep chickens. Her grandmother became sick and Rose Red had to find a way to pay their rent. She did as her grandmother had taught her and made mittens and gloves, knitting on sticks and using fabric from old clothes she unravelled and dyed with food scraps in the pot on the flame in their room. As the cold closed in her grandmother's cough became worse. Rose Red went out every day with her basket, going in and out of inns and stopping people on the street to sell her gloves.

One day she came home half frozen from walking the streets to find a stranger in her grandmother's bed. In a deep and gravelly voice the stranger invited her to stay, licking his lips and tellen her he'd look after her just as well as her grandmother had.

And that was how Rose Red learned her grandmother had died during the long day she'd been away. The landlords had rented the room before her grandmother's body was even cold. The stranger told Rose it was his room now. He was a large man, with a head of black and grey hair that covered most of his face and ran down onto his chest as well, as Rose Red remembered it. At first she thought he was a wolf. He lay under her grandmother's own patchwork quilt, drawing it up under his bristly chin. Rose Red ran away.

'And soon after that I were lucky to get the apprenticeship with the weaver after he saw me on the street, selling my gloves. He was always looking for workers, and children because they are cheap. The terms were harsh. I were indentured to work for him for ten long years. My labour paid for my room and food, and that's all,' she finished. 'But I made sure I learned everything I could.'

'Any other family?' I asked.

'A father I've only seen once or twice. He works away in the mines and drinks his wages when he comes to the city,' she said flatly.

That caused a shiver to run down my spine. I asked her if she were attached to her life in the city or ifen she'd like to move to the mountains with us. I don't know what answer I'd expected but my heart broke to see the girl's eyes fill with tears as she threw her arms around me sayen, *yes please*, and was I sure? I told her we were always in need of skilled hands and that life in the chateau were a struggle but with less filth and no wolves sneaking into your room.

It seemed that Stoat intended to milk the flying display until everyone in the city had paid to see it. He gave Memma enough catalyst to launch her balloon each day to hover above the square, and then pulled her back before the crowds were satisfied, meaning they'd come again the next day. It reminded me of a terrible time when Little Bear were tied to a stake in the miners' yard. It would be just like that watching Memma's spirit being broken.

'The catalyst will run out sooner than later,' Rose Red observed. 'Then the show will be over. What will happen then?'

None of us knew.

'I'm not going to wait around to find out,' Dog-boy said. 'We gotta do something.'

The hunter reported that the crowds in the square built day by day now that Stoat's men knew what to do to prepare the balloon for flying. The morning preparations went much more smoothly and Memma had little to do but prime her elixir machine and sit in the basket for her short flight. Word spread and people started to travel to the city to see it. Inns and markets did strong trade, and Stoat swelled with pride and profits. He refined the show more and more each day. Now he had several heralds on horns playing together. He sold souvenirs, prints and ribbons and toys. He paid a ringman to excite the audience, making them cheer and count down until the balloon's lift-off. Children wore flying goggles in the street and played in washing baskets until they fell apart. Fox, the mayor, appeared on the stage smiling thinly, pleased to be taking his cut, no doubt.

Dog-boy, disguised as Rose Red, went again to visit Memma. Again she told him that Stoat promised to let her continue on her expedition once he'd made back the money he said it took to transport her balloon to the city and pay for her food and accommodations. Once her debt was paid he would let her go. And she refused again to take my coin, saying she were already indebted and could not become more so.

'She doesn't believe she's a prisoner,' Dog-boy reported, 'because she went with Stoat of her own accord. And she's as stubborn as a donkey when I try an' tell her otherwise.'

'I feel responsible,' I said. 'I don't know how life is in her Restoration but she doesn't seem to see things here as they are. Maybe there are no liars or thieves where she's from, though I find that hard to believe.'

'You could shoot through the tether when she's aloft,' Dog-boy told the hunter. 'And set her free.'

'You could!' I said. 'I've seen you shoot a petal off a daisy. You could easily slice the line with one shot.'

'I'm not shooting over the heads of babes and people in a city square,' the hunter said. 'No chance.'

He had a point and I felt silly for the suggestion.

'I got another idea that doesn't involve any shooting,' Dog-boy said.

Dog-boy in the sewers

>>———→

'No, boy, you can't come. Dogs can't climb ladders and I got a few ahead of me before the night is out.'

Poke laid his head on his paws and snuffed his disappointment.

Rose Red, kneeling on the paving next to the hole Dog-boy had just opened into the sewers under the city, handed him a lamp.

'Got everything?'

Dog-boy patted a satchel slung across his chest. 'All set.'

'And you're sure you know the way?' I asked him, one knee on the cold ground, the other holding Poke's collar soas he didn't dive in after his friend.

'Miss, these sewers to me are like the mountains to you. I can find my way blindfolded.'

'See you at the meeting point,' the hunter said, preparing to slide the heavy stone lid back into place over the hole. 'Just like we talked about.'

'Yessir,' Dog-boy said and started down the ladder.

Jumping off at the bottom he headed down the tunnel, breathing through his mouth until he got used to the smells. It weren't just one bad smell but one of every kind of stench a city can produce. He wore boots now, unlike the old days when he went barefoot or with his toes wrapped in rags, and splashed through the murky water dribbling through the tunnels. He'd insisted on going by himself so he could go fast and not be troubled by anyone getting queasy over the filth. He made the turns, this way and that, without needing to think. If he timed it right, he'd come out under the stage in the square before light. Then it were just a matter of following Rose's instructions.

When it came to fibres and fabrics Rose Red could weave or knot, plait, braid, sew or twist a fibre into any shape or construction. It had been her idea to sabotage the balloon's tether. And she'd invented a way to do it so that it were invisible to Stoat as the rope was let out. She taught Dog-boy how to do it by the fire at the inn. There was as much arguing as teaching between the two of them as he practised. Dog-boy dint take as naturally to knots as he did to making explosive gases, but he kept on trying until Rose said he was ready. In the satchel slung over his shoulder he had a sharp knife, wax and matches.

The last part of his underground journey meant shimmying through a pipe as wide as his shoulders and as greasy as a butcher's floor. It smelled just as bad and even Dog-boy held his breath as he slithered along. Reaching the end he dropped into a wide space and headed for another ladder. This one, if he remembered right, was under the centre of the square where icy cold water dripped through a grate to keep the paving dry underfoot. Using all his wiry strength Dog-boy managed to lift the grate and slide it aside just enough to wriggle through. He found himself underneath the balloon launching stage, just as he'd hoped. Nearby was the reel, the long rope rolled around the drum, ready to spool out and hold Memma's balloon in place. The rope was woven and twisted together in four strands. Finding the balloon end, the one that would be high in the air, Dog-boy worked just as Rose had showed him, splitting each strand of rope, weaving and knotting it back together one strand at a time and then covering it in wax to disguise the cuts. Rose had carefully coloured the wax the same shade at the rope, and had shown Dog-boy a knot that held until pulled at both ends. It had to be strong enough to hold as it was let out but weak enough to give way and release the balloon at the right moment.

It were dark and cramped under the stage, and Dog-boy had to work quickly. He did not want to be under the stage when the day's flying preparations began. He smoothed the dyed wax one last time and then slithered back into the sewers. Just as he'd managed to slide the grate back into place over his head he heard heavy steps on the stage. The preparations for the day's flying were getting underway.

The last part of the plan was the most dangerous. Rose volunteered because she was small enough to blend in with the crowds of children that followed Memma from the inn to her balloon each day, and was not known to Stoat or his men as Dog-boy and the rest of us were.

As Dog-boy climbed back into the tunnels under the square, Rose Red joined the gathering of children waiting for Memma. Soon enough, the aeronaut appeared, flanked by Stoat's men. She looked small and tired, Rose Red told us. She kept her eyes to the ground as if even looking up to the sky would lift her hopes. Getting as close as she could, Rose managed to briefly clasp Memma's hand and press a note into her palm. Memma's fingers closed around it and her gaze flicked toward Rose. There were a moment when their eyes met and Rose claimed Memma gave her a small nod.

The message was as simple as we could make it. Given Memma's strange way of speaking we had to be sure she'd understand. It just said, *Fly to the chateau.*

As the day brightened, a gusty wind sprang up, which were lucky. It would make the tether breaking seem more like an accident. We hoped that once it broke and Memma floated free and disappeared through the clouds, Stoat would be fooled by Rose Red's clever sabotage. He would see the frayed rope end and blame his men for being careless. With any luck, he'd pocket his profits and go back to his mercenary ways without giving Memma another thought.

The hunter and I, along with a fretting Poke, waited outside the city for Dog-boy and Rose Red. We'd climbed on a hillock where we could look down on the city and took turns keeping watch. Soon we saw Rose, not hard to spot with her red hair and skirt, climbing up toward us, carrying what looked like a heavy pack on her back.

She'd become part of our family in our short time together, arguing incessantly with Dog-boy like they'd known each other for years. And now here she was, lugging her hard-earned weaving tools on her back, ready for her new life.

'Where is he?' I worried out loud, scanning the roads leading north toward us.

It turned out that Dog-boy had done exactly what we decided – what he'd promised – he should not do. That which we'd all agreed was too risky, that if he were caught would throw us all back into trouble with Stoat.

But he'd done it anyway. Instead of squirming his way through the underground water and sewer tunnels to the edge of the city where he'd emerge well out of sight and be able to run up to our meeting point without anyone noticing, Dog-boy wriggled to a nearby stormwater drain and squeezed out into the open square. Squatting in a doorway, he wrapped a scarf around his whole face, just leaving his one good eye to see through a slit. And then he waited.

Everyone who made the mistake of coming close quickly changed course when they smelled him. He did not react to any of the insults that came his way from the well-dressed people of the city. Instead he thought to himself that even the smelliest pigs were better people than those who abused a person just for sitting in a doorway stinking.

He sat still and waited as Memma was escorted to her basket and watched her fuel the elixir machine with the ration of catalyst Stoat gave her, and he watched closely as the balloon started to rise and Memma let out the sand in her weights and it blew around the square in whirly-whirlies, stinging the eyes of those watching. He kept a close eye on the rope and was pleased that he could not see at all where he had so carefully sabotaged it. And most of all he watched as the balloon reached its full height, tugging at the end of the line, the wind gusts coming a little more strongly now, just as we'd hoped. Each gust of wind would weaken the rope, causing the knots to part way one by one.

However the timing now was delicate. The rope needed to give before Stoat called to his men to wind the balloon in. If they began winding before the rope gave, Memma might crash into the roofs and spires of the buildings in the square.

It had to give as she floated at the very end of the rope. With his sharp eye Dog-boy kept a close watch on the sabotaged end and hoped for more wind gusts.

Stoat ordered his heralds to play as the balloon strained at the tether. It seemed to Dog-boy that the craft tugged impatiently at the tie like a child with her bootlace snagged in a grate.

Memma leaned over the basket, scanning the crowd. It were too far to catch her eye but Dog-boy hoped she saw him, though what she saw, if anything, would look more like a pile of rags in a doorway than a young man. A large gust of wind threw up more sand and snow from the paving, causing the crowd to cover their eyes and turn their backs to it like cows in a field. Skirts were being picked up and scarves and hats caught and sent flying. Grit flew into the food carts and the mood turned irritable. The crowd on the ground became preoccupied with their own discomfort and not even the heralds and their horn-playing could recapture a festive mood.

At that moment, Dog-boy saw that Stoat was about to signal an end to the display.

Memma needed more time. He stood quickly and crossed the corner of the square, stopping at the bottom of the council steps. As he hoped, Stoat descended to give the order to his men. Dog-boy bounced up and ran past him, as if involved in a game of chase with an invisible partner. He bumped heavily into Stoat's legs, the larger man reeling back in horror.

'Blasted beggar, watch where you go!'

But Dog-boy had managed to become entangled with Stoat's long scarf.

'Get off me!' Stoat yelled, pushing Dog-boy away and pulling at his scarf to get it back at the same time. 'Away, you stinking rat-dog!'

Stoat's men were reluctant to lay their hands on such a vile-smelling creature, but soon Dog-boy disentangled himself and disappeared down the nearest alley. Stoat made much of throwing the tainted scarf to the ground and brushing himself off.

In the kerfuffle, Memma floated free.

The first Stoat knew of it was the tethering rope falling to the stage in heavy loops, the frayed end landing on top. Stoat's gaze went first to the rope and then to the balloon which was already rising rapidly toward the cover of the clouds. The wind was blowing strongly and the basket rocked from side to side but Memma, a tiny figure now up very high, adjusted straps and pulled on ropes skilfully until the silks tautened and the basket steadied.

'Come back, madame!' Stoat yelled. 'Land that balloon, on my orders!'

And then finally, as the balloon continued to rise and Memma became a speck in the sky, he shouted, 'You won't get far without the catalyst!'

However, upon searching his coat, Stoat could not find the box of powdered metal. It no longer sat snug in his pocket, keeping Memma tethered as much as the rope. It was gone, and so was the balloon.

Dog-boy reached us as dark was falling.

'Where you been? Heck, boy, you smell as bad as month-old guts. You'll be keeping downwind of us, ifen you please,' the hunter told him.

Dog-boy, unable to keep it to himself, pulled out the box of catalyst.

'I got this. Just in case,' he said, proudly showing us.

The hunter were furious. 'But now you've given it away, Dog-boy. We talked about this. The sabotage kept us out of it. Now you've gone and pick-pocketed him and he's gonna put two and two together and find that it equals a bad-smelling, one-eyed boy.'

Dog-boy shrugged. 'He dint see it were me. I coulda been any street rat pickpocket. And I dint just take the box. I also got this. And this,' he said, emptying his pockets to show us a large bag of city coin and a golden watch that looked to be brand new.

The hunter rubbed his face and shook his head. 'Boy . . .'

I saw Dog-boy and Rose Red exchange a long look that seemed to hold a whole discussion.

'What?' I said. 'What's going on?'

'It's a grand scheme that int ready to talk about just yet, miss,' Dog-boy said.

'More of an idea than a plan, if we're being honest,' Rose Red added.

For once, Dog-boy agreed with her. 'That's right, really more of a theory than an idea even. But we'll need all the catalyst if it's to have a hope of working.'

We were wasting time. 'Hurry,' I told them. 'We've got to run. It's the chateau by morning if we're quick. I want some high walls and heavy gates between us and Stoat if he has a mind to follow. We'll discuss this later.'

PART II

A grand scheme

It dint take long to find out what Dog-boy had been hinting at.

Even though we raced up the mountain from the city after Memma's release, we arrived well after she'd made her graceful descent, landing softly in the chateau bailey to everyone's astonishment. The watchman reestablished some calm and welcomed Memma back and, with difficulty, eventually understood that the hunter and I were following but may be quite a way behind, balloon travel being somewhat faster than foot.

There had been no sign we were being followed, yet all the same I ordered the gates locked behind us.

We trudged into the warm hall and peeled off our coats and boots, wriggling frozen toes to warm them by the fire. It had been a cold hard walk and I'd never been happier to be safe again. Memma descended the main stairs, hesitating on the bottom one like she weren't sure if she were welcome among us. But Dog-boy drew her in and returned her catalyst strongbox to her with some ceremony. Sitting on a stool in front of the great hall fire and resting her head in her hands, Memma gazed at the box sitting safely in her lap. She were very grateful, she told us, her blue, bird-like eyes filling with tears, to be free to continue on her way.

'Sooner the better, in fact,' the hunter said quietly, thinking of a furious Stoat charging up the mountain.

'And these too,' I said, digging in my pocket for the fire-mountain coins. 'Dog-boy discovered they are made of the catalyst, so you should have them for extra fuel. I'll just keep one as a keepsake,' I added.

Memma peered at the coins and then turned her sharp gaze on me. 'Whence did thee find these, child?'

I was defensive under her scrutiny. 'From my mother in her tomb. My real mother that is.'

'Bid thee tell me the story of thy birth, if thee please,' Memma asked.

'Int much to tell,' I said, embarrassed. 'She were a Voyager, people say. Arrived by sea before it froze over. And rejected by her people. She made her way to the chateau and died having me. My father and his wife adopted me. Then she died as well and along came my nasty stepmother.'

I couldn't read Memma's expression. 'That's all I know,' I finished.

'You know what this means, Memma. You can continue on your expedition now,' Dog-boy told her.

But Memma was hesitant. 'Thou hath been kind and shown help to me beyond what I couldst ev'r hath desired. I feeleth for thee all in this terrible frozen land. I want to offer my help in resolving your quandary.'

This were a long talk in Memma's strange language and we looked to each other for a moment in confusion. Dog-boy was the first to catch on.

'She wants to stay,' he said, eyes wide.

Rose Red jumped up and down in excitement, setting Poke off barking.

'Shush, Poke,' I told him. 'Memma, are you sure? It would be safest for you to take to the skies at the earliest chance. Don't you want to go home?'

Memma was sure.

'Then, madame, we have a lot we need to learn from you.'

With this, Dog-boy and Rose Red, each holding one of Memma's arms, took her up the stairs to the library.

'What's all that about?' wondered the hunter.

I was so weary I were about to lie down and fall asleep right there on the floor. 'I suppose we're about to find out.'

After a few days shut away in the library, this time drafting diagrams and cutting patterns and making mess with pine needles, the mister, Memma, Dog-boy and Rose Red had masterminded a grand scheme, thought through from all angles. They had tested their theory with calculations and observations and measurements from Memma's travels. The results of their work were announced in the great hall.

The scraps of a meal lay around us on the long tables, eaten hurriedly by people keen to hear the announcement. The fires burned warm and dogs and goats lay on their sides dozing on full stomachs. The birds watched from perches in the rafters above us. Candles and lamps cast a warm glow on the company assembled. Memma began to explain.

'From what I hath learned, this history hast been forgotten on this island, but according to the records of the Restoration, the most disastrous quake of five generations ago did cause the eruption of the volcano lies yond north. The gases and dust releas'd in that vast explosion opened the Little Ice Age noweth continuing into a fourth generation. Ev'r since yond volcano, which thee named fire-mountain, hast been erupting, the steady stream of ash pouring into the atmosphere hast caused the buildeth up of permanent stratus cover, hence obscuring the stars. Two winters ago, at which hour the clouds did part briefly – coincidentally at the same time as Snow awaken'd from a coma induced by bitter cold and her injury – thither hadst been a heavy precipitation – rain. 'Tis seemeth, from the studies I hath conducted, this moisture temporarily dampen'd the erupting volcano, causing a break in the atmospheric dust, and the sun to appeareth. Anon, the surveys I hath done from the air before my hard landing hast reveal'd a frozen lake that sits in the ancient crater of a volcano. 'Tis at present dammed by glaciers but, in theory, if 't be true, we can heat the dam and form a free-flowing riv'r. The course of the riv'r would cross a fissure in the side of the fire-mountain and, pouring in, beginneth to quell the fire yond burns within. If 't be true we can cause another break in the clouding o'er, as 'tis known in these parts, the sun shall continueth the worketh we did start, warming yond lake, melting the glacier and increasing the riv'r flow, further dampening the volcanic reaction and, with some luck, ending the Little Ice Age and returning solar warmth to the whole earth.'

'We melt a lake and put out a fire, basically,' Dog-boy summarised.

He'd been interpreting Memma's long speech for those who found her difficult to follow, and finished a moment or two after she did.

I surveyed the shocked expressions of the assembly, sure my face looked exactly the same as those around me. I asked the question that was on everyone's minds. 'And how do we melt a lake?'

'We maketh a giant silk tent o'er the dam and heat up the air inside, just like a balloon,' Memma replied.

'Oh,' I said weakly. 'Of course.'

'And how do we get there?' the hunter asked.

'We make a fleet of balloons to carry us!' Dog-boy said, jumping out of his skin in excitement.

'And where will the fuel to heat a giant dome come from?'

'We shall useth the elixir engine,' Memma replied. 'We hath enough fuel from the strongbox and the coins combin'd, along with the burners from yond hot-air balloons.'

'The fleet balloons will have plain fuel burners, not elixir machines,' Dog-boy said. 'They don't fly as far, but far enough to carry us to fire-mountain.'

'And how will you get home then, madame?' the hunter asked.

The heads of everyone in the whole group swung from the hunter to Memma.

'I shall be'est stranded, 'tis true. But thither isn't any people I'd rather be'est strand'd 'mongst than those I see afore me,' Memma said, her eyes bright.

'Besides, once the sky is open and the seas turn to water again, we can build a boat and float her home that way,' Dog-boy said, throwing an arm around Memma's shoulders.

The hunter and I looked at each other. This was the Grandest of Schemes. The grandest I'd ever heard.

Cook raised her hand. 'Every time I've ever poured water

on a fire all it does is make a mess of smoke and steam,' she said. 'How do we know there's enough water in the lake to put out a fire burning in the belly of a mountain without making matters worse?'

Memma raised her pointed chin a little. 'We don't knoweth. 'Tis all a theory. Bas'd on accurate observations, 'tis true, but still, we don't knoweth.'

Cook went on. 'And if the lake is melted and the fire is dampened, how will you get my loved ones home again?' she asked. 'I hope you're not proposing to maroon everyone I've ever held dear in my heart on a mountain top.'

'The balloon silks will be reassembled and we'll fly home, Cook. No fretting,' Dog-boy said.

'Humph,' was Cook's reply. 'If you're wrong, boy, you won't need to worry about a rescue because I'll come up that mountain to find you and paddle your backside with my biggest wooden spoon.'

Dog-boy grinned in reply.

I stood, putting my hands on my hips. 'When do we leave?'

A cheer went up in the hall.

'We wait f'r the weather,' Memma said.

'So it could be a while then,' said the hunter quietly.

The silk balloons

The weaving room was buzzing when I reported for my shift. It occupied one of the largest sheds within the chateau walls and had fallen into disrepair, as had everything, during my stepmother's time. The last person to work there was the hunter's mother after she arrived on the mountain running from trouble in the city. That were a long time ago when I was a wee thing hiding under Cook's table and the hunter was a boy wearing his dead father's too-big boots. The hunter's mother had passed away since and the weaving room had become dusty and overrun with cobwebs and mice.

Rose Red pulled open the doors and gasped, and it were hard to tell whether it was in horror or excitement. I rushed to tell her we'd get people in to dust and sweep away the mouse mess, that the broken windows could be repaired, but she was too busy passing among the giant looms, running her hand over the mechanisms, and skipping between each machine.

'And this is really all for me?' she said. 'I mean, for me to fix and get working again?'

I assured her that if she had the will to do it, it was all hers. I left her examining some huge copper dye pots and cautiously poking the brick fireplaces underneath, and went back to the library.

After Memma's speech all spare hands were summoned and work rosters drawn up. There would be teams at work on basket construction, fabric and fuel manufacture and rope weaving.

Our balloons would be different to Memma's. They would work with plain hot air, not hydrogen. This meant they couldn't fly as far or as high, but there would be no need for a catalyst or the machine for making the gas. We would make bricks of fuel from a mixture of animal dung, fatwood dust and beeswax.

The balloon would be made from silk and the silk would be made by worms. In the heavy pack she'd brought with her from the city, carrying them all the way on our fast march up the mountain, Rose had packed her essential working tools which, I were astonished to discover, included a box of worms.

Rose Red had her weavers toiling on the silk looms late into the nights, making the vast volume of fabric we'd need. I was assigned to look after the silk worms which were kept in a small room warmed by the fires kept lit under the dye pots. Making my way through the snapping and clicking weaving looms, keeping my fingers clear of the mechanisms and minding I didn't trip on any loose threads, I slipped into the quiet of the worm room. Caring for the insects wasn't that different to looking after goats, only they weren't likely to kick you if they weren't pleased with your milking. They were really caterpillars. And calling them worms I felt was an insult to these clever creatures who ate their way through leaves, growing to the size of my thumb, before spinning themselves into a cocoon. Once the silk moths had emerged and laid their eggs, they were released into the cold air above the bailey, their work done. Then the strands of the caterpillar's silk cocoon were carefully separated and spun into very light and strong fabric.

The baskets were also being woven, but from pine needles. This was done by teams that hurried out through the gates under guard and completed their harvesting work in haste. The hunter supervised their trips, hurrying them along so as they weren't outside for long in the cold and just in case Stoat was waiting for a chance to pay an unwelcome visit. The pine needles were dried on great racks near the fires and then woven tightly into frames to make baskets.

There was a moment in the midst of all this effort and toil when the hunter and I crossed paths in the bailey. I were lugging another basket of leaves for the hungry silk worms and he were splitting logs for the oven baking our fuel bricks. Our eyes met and he straightened, resting his axe on his foot. I swung my plait over my shoulder and he smiled at me. My cheeks went red and it weren't the cold. Sometimes there were no need for words between us. Though we were hard at work our bond was always there, running deep.

The long nights set in while we were hard at work. The cold descended along with the dark. Lamps were lit at midday and those responsible for keeping the chateau fires burning were worn thin by the task of collecting, cutting, stacking, drying and carrying the wood. If just surviving wasn't enough work, making a fleet of balloons made a lot more. But the project seemed to give hope to not only those who were working in Rose Red's weaving shed, or those making the fuel bricks, or the basket weavers, but also everyone else who were occupied with the everyday chores. Just like we'd seen in the city, balloons entered everyone's dreams. Children played balloons in the bailey and drew pictures of Memma and her flying craft in their lessons. It was the topic of the adults' conversations as well as they went about their work. What would it be like above the clouds? What would it feel like to float so high above solid ground? What had happened in the night sky since we'd seen it last? Were all the same stories playing out in the clusters of stars up there? People started remembering the fables and telling them again. The ones about stars shaped like animals and those that looked like families or saucepans or ships in sail.

Ifen I were honest I dint much like overhearing these conversations because they made me feel queasy. While I was eager for the adventure, I was less enthusiastic about my feet leaving solid ground. I practised facing my fears by climbing the east tower and leaning out the windows there, putting my face in the cold wind and shutting my eyes to imagine floating up out of reach of the tops of trees, as high as birds fly.

One day, as I leaned out of the window, feeling silly, but determined to overcome my jelly legs as best I could, I were startled by cheeping. In the tower wall there was a nest in a hollow made by a missing stone or two. Among the sticks softened by flax were three chicks, still with their fluffy feathers, all looking to me like I were about to produce a worm for their dinner. A moment or two later, their real mother alighted gracefully on the very edge of the hollow, eyeing me in warning. She had red-brown feathers around her thighs, long tawny brown wings and horizontal stripes across her tail feathers. She held a mouse in her curved beak and turned her back on me, spreading her wings protectively while feeding it to her chicks.

After that I often climbed the tower steps, eager to check on the hawklets. I gave them names though the hunter told me I shouldn't. Tyke, because he liked to hop dangerously close to the edge of the nest, Zephyr for the wind that always blew at the top of the tower, and Lady for her regal tolerance of her brothers. It would be months before they were ready to fly and I felt we had that in common. Over the weeks their baby feathers fledged into the tawny grey-brown colouring of young birds and their cries for food grew louder and more insistent. I hoped they wouldn't leave before the balloons were ready. Their taking flight and my first flight came to be mixed up in my head, though I dint doubt theirs would be more graceful.

A long, hard storm

Rose Red and Dog-boy often argued but one day they stormed into the kitchen demanding I settle a dispute. It was bread day and I had been helping Cook with the kneading, sleeves rolled to the elbow, fingers sticky with dough, enjoying the crackle of the fire in the big old stove and Cook's easy company. I heard the bickering as they made their way along the upstairs hallway, down the main stairs and through the corridors to the back of the house where the kitchen lay.

'Making them pretty is a waste of time and effort,' I heard Dog-boy say.

'Seeing as it's entirely my effort and not yours, I don't see the problem,' Rose Red fired back.

'Ifen it slows down the manufacture while you stick on ribbons and sparkles, then it becomes my problem.'

'*Ribbons and sparkles!*'

Though I couldn't see, I imagined Rose Red's cheeks popping with indignation, but she reined in her temper.

'It won't slow anyone down any. I got it all worked out, Dog-boy. Your precious schedule won't be broken. The dye is added to the boiling, so it doesn't add any time at all, and then the weavers make the patterns without any trouble. Anyway, why should I explain anything to you? I'm in charge of the silks, so it's up to me how they're finished.'

'You're in charge of the silks, but I'm overseeing the whole fleet,' Dog-boy said.

I winced.

'And there we have it!' Rose Red said, dripping sarcasm. 'He thinks he's the boss of everyone. I hate to burst your bubble of pride, Dog-boy, but this is a team effort. Everyone doing their part, and you are not the chairman or president or king of anything!'

'I dint say I was,' Dog-boy said sulkily.

'Yes, you did! You *just* did!' Rose Red sang as they arrived in the kitchen. 'Miss Snow,' she went on, breathless from the brisk walk through the big house while using most of her lungs in yelling. 'Can you please tell Big Head that it isn't up to him to say whether or not I make the balloons look beautiful so long as it doesn't delay or slow down the making of the silks?'

Just then a particularly strong gust of wind rattled the roof and sent something stacked in the bailey tumbling over. There was shouting and doors banging open and shut in the gale.

We all glanced to the roof, hoping the rusty nails and patched holes held.

'Seeing as it looks like no one's going anywhere in a balloon any time soon, Dog-boy, I'd say Rose has time to embroider the silk by hand if she has a mind to,' I told them.

Rose Red turned triumphantly to Dog-boy.

'However,' I continued. 'I believe, Rose, you owe Dog-boy an apology for calling attention to the size of his head.'

'Sorry,' Rose told him. 'It's beneath me to resort to personal insults.'

Dog-boy looked sheepish. 'And I'm sorry about inflating my role. I'm probably more like a coordinator than commander.'

Rose Red rolled her eyes.

'Have you solved the problem of scorch-proofing the neck of the envelopes?' I asked them. This had been the topic of discussion at dinner.

'Ah! I had an idea about that,' Rose Red said.

'What was it?' Dog-boy replied as they turned and hurried back upstairs to the library, the grand scheme nerve centre, their argument forgotten, for now.

I paused in my kneading and looked to Cook. 'Ten times a day that happens! It's going to be a long, long night.'

Cook chuckled and clanged open the oven. 'Reminds me of a couple of wee'ns I once knew before they worked out their differences.'

I took it she meant me and the hunter. 'I'd best check on whatever that crash was,' I said, dusting flour from my hands and pulling on boots.

Outside, a section of the goats' shed had been ripped away. The hunter was already there, heavy gloves on and a scarf tied around his face. The gale was bitterly cold and icy rain fell in sheets that burned any skin that were left exposed. I crossed the bailey, leaning into the wind, to lend a hand. The goats had been pushed against the far wall, bleating in fright. I went to them and tried to calm them while the builder, a woman named Gorrie, assessed the damage.

'Best move them somewhere dry,' she shouted to me over the noise. 'Int any repair happening in this gale.'

Taking the old lady nanny with me by one horn, I pulled her toward the weaving shed which were the nearest shelter, just across the yard. Pulling my hood up and holding my scarf across my face with my free hand, I staggered the few paces, glancing back to see that the rest of the herd were following close. I pulled open the door, letting in a swirl of ice and snow and put my back against it to hold it open as the goats filed through, skittery after their fright. The hunter came last, crossing the courtyard in long strides with a frightened kid under each arm.

'It's bad,' I said, as I unwound my scarf, shoulder to the closed door as the hunter struggled with the latch against the wind.

'As bad as it gets,' he replied.

It looked like it would be one of those nights when the two of us stayed awake, alert for damage and flooding or fires from sparks in chimneys. There would be no sleep anyway with the racket of the wind and ice pelting the windows. We'd have to wait it out, like all the other storms we'd stood watch through together.

Gorrie and her builders gathered in the kitchen in the pre-dawn dark.

'The roof of the chicken coop has been ripped off,' she told us, stamping her feet in her boots to warm them, fingers wrapped around a steaming mug of tea.

'The chickens?' I asked.

'All gone,' she replied, shaking her head sadly. 'Ripped off their perches and flung into the high heavens.'

This was bad news. 'And the west tower?' I asked.

'Be a miracle if it holds up, through this,' Gorrie said.

The west tower was the one my stepmother had locked me in when I were a girl, and if I'm telling the truth, I'd deliberately neglected its upkeep over the years since. Gradually the roof had fallen in which let the snow and ice into the mortar and it had quickly gone to ruin. Our worry was that in its weakened state it would fall onto the buildings below in a storm like this, which would be a disaster. I could've kicked myself for my cowardly neglect. Lives were now in danger, all because I dint like to mount the stairs and face my fears to repair the roof.

'Int only your fault, Snow. The place holds bad memories for others as well,' the hunter said, reading my expression.

'Next break in the weather, we'll take it apart stone by stone and rebuild lower and stronger,' Gorrie promised. 'But until then, it's waiting and hoping it holds up.'

We fell silent as the gale strengthened. Even the strong stone walls of the main house seemed to shift and groan under the assault.

'I'm going to shovel out the cellar again,' I said, pulling on my gloves.

'I'll come,' the hunter said, rising to his feet.

There was a small hole in the wall of the food cellar, where a vent used to be, and whenever the wind blew, everything in the cellar gradually became covered in a thick layer of ice and snow. I was just getting hold of a shovel when we heard a dull thud followed by a huge crash.

'The west tower,' I said, full of dread.

The hunter was already running in that direction.

Pushing through the thigh-deep snow to cross the bailey, one hand as always on the guide rope that ran between buildings, it was so dark and the ice-storm so thick that we could not see our way at all. We crossed by memory and found Gorrie by running into her. By feeling our way and getting glimpses by the dim light of our lanterns, we saw that mercies granted, it wasn't the west tower that had collapsed but a section of the wall at its base. The snow had been so banked up against it that it had fallen in. Within hours, perhaps sooner, the bailey would be filled with snow and all the greenhouses and animal yards buried, not to mention all the doors snowed-in and windows covered.

For the rest of the night all able hands were summoned to shovel snow away from the main buildings. It were too cold to stay outside for long, even with the work to keep warm, so people worked in short shifts. Gorrie, heroically, managed some temporary repairs to the wall, enough to stop snow blowing through, and eventually it started banking up on the outside of the wall again. By then the short day was over, not that it had been noticeable. Dawn had come and it was easier to see, the snow glowing white, and then the pale light faded again, and everything was black.

By the time the gale eased, the snow still falling, but the worst of the wind slackening, my hands were frozen and blistered. I staggered into the kitchen and collapsed on the long bench, exhausted. I were so tired I dint feel cold anymore, just like I needed to sleep. Dog-boy, bless him, saw I were half-frozen, and he and Rose Red pulled off my wet coat and scarf and tucked warm stones into my hands. Slowly I thawed out. Those worse off than me were tucked under mounds of blankets and were having their hands and feet massaged to coax back the blood.

'We can't go on like this,' I croaked.

The hunter, his beard turned white with ice, the tip of his nose bright red with cold, said, 'This is surviving, Snow. This is what we do.'

I were too tired to argue and put my head on the table, falling into an exhausted sleep.

Sickness in the chateau

The relentless storm that long night season weren't our only trouble. As the wind howled around the walls and the icy rain pelted the chateau roofs, Cook found us, coming through the kitchen door with a swirl of snow and ice like she had a fiend on her heels.

'There's sickness in the main dormitory, Snow,' she told me, filling the kettle and setting it on the stove. 'One family taken ill. Two wee'ns and their mother. Some others coughing.'

This news sent chills right through me, ifen the endless storm weren't enough to be jangling my nerves.

'Too many sleeping in the same room,' I said, glancing toward the hunter.

'Can't be helped,' he said.

'Cook, please move them into our room for now. We're not using our bed while this gale keeps up. And anyone else feeling ill should also move out. Last thing we want is sickness running through the whole place.'

Memma appeared in the doorway. She wore a long gown instead of her flying suit and her white hair fell around her shoulders. Her face was creased with sleep. She'd heard the last part of our conversation. 'There is an illness 'mongst the people? Dost thou hath a physic?'

'No doctor. Just Cook,' the hunter said curtly.

'What about tests, medicines, a hospital?'

'None of those,' I replied before the hunter could jump in again. 'We have remedies to treat fever and infections,' I added. 'But our ways are simple, Memma.'

'Finding out the name of the disease doesn't matter much when the treatment is always the same: hot tea and rest and quarantine,' Cook added.

I went with Cook to move the family, going the long way around to the main dormitory soas to stay out of the storm. It were possible, we'd made it so, to walk between most buildings along cloisters that kept us out of the weather.

On our way back I carried the baby and Cook helped the mother along. Her partner carried the other child. Three others had admitted to feeling unwell and so we brought them with us too. Settled soon after in rooms to themselves soas not to spread the illness to others, they were comfortable enough when we left them, hot water bottles and pots of Cook's tea close to hand.

'If anyone else gets sick we'll have to find more room,' I told the hunter when we returned to the kitchen.

'Search me for where,' he said. 'There's already goats in the weaving room.'

'The hall, if need be. We can move the long tables. And after that the library. Dog-boy will have to spread his charts and schedules out somewhere else. Memma, you should go back to your room and keep your distance from us now.'

'Thou wilt care for the sick?' she asked.

'As best we can,' was my reply. 'You go too,' I told the hunter. But he refused. 'Too late now. We been breathing the same air these last few minutes and if there's people to move, I'll lend a hand. Int anything else can be done right now.'

Over the next few days many fell ill. We kept a strict divide between those showing symptoms and those who were still well, but even so the infection spread quickly. The hall filled up with sick beds and the library as well. Dog-boy and Rose Red moved the balloon-making to the weaving room and slept there with the goats and Memma.

The hunter, Cook and I tended the sick. The illness began with a fever and aches, and sometimes there was a rash as well, mostly on the children. After a couple of days, thank goodness, the children recovered but for some adults their tongues and throats became painfully swollen and sore. It was hard to get them to drink and we became gravely worried.

The hunter fell ill after several days, having run himself down with hard work over the last few months. He were forced to lie down on a cot in the corner of the library, surrounded by the sick. Everyone sleeping and groaning and suffering together. I nursed those in the library while Cook covered the hall. The kitchen stove boiled water for tea around the clock.

The hunter was a difficult patient, there was no surprise there. Every time I'd come to pull up his blankets and pause a minute to hold his hand he'd send me away, telling me he were fine and others were in more need than he. When he was asleep I sat by him, my gaze resting on the familiar lines in a face I'd known for most of my life. He twitched in his sleep as fevers brought him bad dreams. I smoothed them away as best I could by stroking the worry lines from his brow. 'Don't leave me, hunter,' I whispered. 'You said you never would again, remember?'

I had more time with him as gradually people started to recover. The children first, mercies granted, and then the younger people and finally the older ones, who took the infection the hardest. The hunter was one of the last to rise from his sickbed. He did so one day as I was folding blankets and dragging mattresses out of the library. I found him sitting on the edge of his bed, weak and pale from the effort of sitting up.

'You need food and rest,' I told him, hugging him tight. 'Remember you caught a wild goat in the mountains to help me get stronger after being frozen to death?'

He smiled at me.

'But no need to run this time, so you can lie down a while longer,' I told him.

'Maybe just one more day,' he mumbled, lying down and letting me cover him.

The storm eased as well, slowly. No one could remember one lasting as long. On the first calm day I counted a whole month had passed since the gale had set in. Taking in the damage, Gorrie discovered a few chickens wedged under their nestbox and covered in snow. They were dug out, hungry and indignant, and given warm porridge.

Finally the hunter started to walk around, as wobbly as a newborn kid.

'We gotta build more accommodation,' he told me when I found him.

'One grand scheme at a time,' I said.

'Keeping sickness out of the house is more important than

chasing after balloons. If these are the new storms, then we int prepared.'

'I agree, but we've only got so many hands,' I told him. 'Anyway, we made it through. And no one died, thanks be. No one at all. If it happens again we'll do the same and hope for the best.'

Flying school begins

While we waited out the dark season, Memma and the mister set up a flying school. The great hall was the only space large enough, so the long tables were once again set back against the walls to make room. The baskets were being finished one by one. Shaped like baths, just the same as Memma's, they were designed for one person. Finely and tightly woven from pine needles, they were light and sturdy. This, Memma said, would mean the whole craft could be small and manoeuvrable, as much as a balloon can be flown, rather than blown, Memma added. Each craft was fitted with a set of wings toward the back. Memma's basket had a propeller and a tiller because she had power to spare from her elixir machine. Our balloons would be steered – and again Memma told us, as much as it were possible to steer a balloon – by these clever little wings raised and lowered by the pilot using levers.

We were all pilots. Memma insisted on calling us such, and us calling each other. *Ahoy there, Pilot Dog-boy! Received loud and clear, Pilot Snow!*

Our pilot training began when the hall had been fitted out with an ingenious system of ropes and pulleys attached to the baskets and looped up over the huge beams that held up the roof. A representation of the sun rising in the east and setting in the west had been painted on a huge round of fabric and stretched on a frame above the rafters in the hall. Rose Red stitched a golden sun with a warm halo that had the effect of spreading warmth across the large room. With the pull of a few ropes, another chart showing the constellations could be drawn across the sun, turning day to night. It made a beautiful decoration and I saw no need to take it down once we had learned our lessons. Across the floor a map of the whole land had been painstakingly drawn in chalk from old maps, showing the land and the sea around us, all the way into the frozen south. As the basket was hoisted, the pilot could look down on the mountains and rivers below, and above to the sun or stars moving across the sky.

We had to learn to use the sun and stars to find our way. We also had to master flying: how to keep our balloons aloft with hot air, how to lose weight to rise, and release hot air to descend. And if that weren't enough to burst my head open, at the same time we'd have to read the weather so we could avoid storms.

Reading the weather were the only part of it all that I felt I had a grip on until Memma told us that the weather is completely different above the clouds. Up high the air moves in rivers that are fast and slow and sometimes cross each other. Some clouds are harmless and others hold lightning, though they might look almost the same.

On the first day of flying school, Dog-boy climbed into his basket while the other pilots-in-training watched. Our balloon fleet would be five balloons strong: me, the hunter, Dog-boy, and Rose Red, plus Memma. Poke would be left behind, which he hadn't been officially told just yet, but he seemed to have his suspicions as he watched Dog-boy climb into the basket which was then raised into the air. He circled underneath, barking, reminding Dog-boy that he'd forgotten something. We called him to wait with us and he put his nose on his paws and settled into a deep sulk.

The basket swung in circles while Memma shouted her flying instructions. Gorrie had built a raised platform, accessed by a ladder, so that the scientist-aeronaut could observe the pilot. She also had a series of ropes she could pull on to simulate situations we'd likely have to deal with. But for now, all she said was for Dog-boy to release his ballast and rise to cruising altitude. Dog-boy, for once without arguing, released the bags of sand around his basket and the simulation team hauled him off the floor until he hung level with Memma's platform.

Among Memma's controls were levers for spinning the sky map so that her pilots had to find their guiding star or the sun. Memma knew them all by heart but we were new to learning their whereabouts in the sky. And we needed to know how to sail the balloon across the wind, using the wings. Sometimes the wind direction changed at different altitudes, Memma patiently explained to us. But this was good news because by descending or ascending we could control where we flew.

Having reached cruising altitude, as Memma called it, Dog-boy began to work through his checklist.

I was learning that everything about flying was a list. And sometimes items on the list had their own lists. We watched as Dog-boy checked his burner, loaded in more fuel, trimmed his wings, tested the rope that led to the release valve at the top of the envelope, and finally called, 'All checks completed.'

Memma hit the lever that sent the star chart spinning above and after a few seconds locked it down again. Like a child's top it never dropped in the same place twice, so it was different for every pilot, just as it would be if we'd come through a storm and been twisted and turned around.

'Set a northerly course, pilot,' Memma said.

We watched as Dog-boy craned his neck to look at the star chart above him. He soon found what he was looking for, the bright diamond-shaped group of four stars in the southern sky. Nearby he found two more stars, close together. Holding his arms out straight, Dog-boy drew a line in the sky downwards. He'd found south. Turning his back on south he pointed his body the opposite way, north.

'Valorous effort!' called Memma. 'Now, initiate steering.'

Dog-boy, frowning in concentration, placed both hands on the levers in the basket controlling the wings, depressing one side and lifting the other. With no strong winds in the great hall, the simulation was completed with assistants, turning the basket with ropes into position on Dog-boy's new heading.

We could see Memma frowning. 'Check your course again, pilot,' she shouted.

Dog-boy, carefully soas not to bump his wings, turned to look over his shoulder at the constellation and saw that he'd oversteered. Turning back to his levers, he adjusted his wing tilt slightly.

'Simulation over, pilot,' Memma called out.

Turning to a chalkboard, she wrote up Dog-boy's results. She gave marks out of ten in a series of categories, none of them over six.

Dog-boy was lowered to the floor of the hall, looking grumpy.

'Sixes!' he said to Poke. 'Dint crash, did I?'

'Next pilot, taketh thy seat,' called Memma.

Flying school was the hardest learning I'd ever done. Harder than learning to read and write when I was no longer a child. Harder than when I had to teach myself to cook and clean for a miners' camp. And it wasn't because I dint have a feel for the weather or the controls of the balloon, my problem was that I couldn't memorise the checklists. There was a pre-flight check, a flight check, a navigation protocol and a descent procedure. Plus all the flags we'd use to talk to each other when it were too far to shout. Dog-boy and Rose Red, being younger and nimbler in their thinking, memorised it all easily. Me and the hunter were struggling to tell one checklist from another, let alone have them all straight. We both pulled our hair out in frustration every day. Memma insisted that the checks be done from memory and in exact order. I could see the sense in that, so that no important step was missed out, but when it was my turn in the simulator my marks were threes and fours. The hunter was the same except he were likely to lose his temper and start throwing his checklists overboard.

Soon Rose Red and Dog-boy weren't even looking at their written lists anymore and their scores were higher every day.

The hunter and I climbed to the top of the east tower to check on the hawklets and study our lists in peace. Reading the checklists and reciting them over and over just wasn't working, for either of us. Losing my patience, I went to lean out of the window. For once the wind wasn't blowing a gale and no snow was falling. The world outside the chateau was silent. A thick bed of fresh drift was higher up the outside walls than I'd ever seen it, as if the ground was rising up to meet the high tower. A few spans away, in the hole in the wall, the hawk was giving her own flying instructions to her chicks. I called the hunter over to look. He happily dropped his flying paperwork to join me.

As we watched, the hawk hopped to the very edge of the nest and began to open her wings. Shifting her weight a little, she let the wind come up underneath so that her wing feathers were filled with air. Keeping her head up, she leaned out a little more, extending her wings this time, letting the air hold her up. After a few breaths, she folded her wings and stepped into the nest, nudging Lady with her beak. Lady stepped carefully to the edge, ignoring the pushing and shoving of her brothers behind her, and copied her mother's technique. Leaning out into open air, opening her wings a little, letting the wind fill out her feathers and then just before the wind took her full weight, stepping back into the nest.

'I got an idea,' I told the hunter.

He raised his eyebrows. 'I'm all ears,' he said. 'I'll do anything to raise my marks above twos. My pride can't take any more.'

I told him to sit, just as he would in the basket, and instead of trying to read off the list, he was to imagine where his hands were for every check. Where his hands were, and then where they moved to. Each check formed part of a dance.

'Just like hunting,' I told him. 'Do you think about all the steps to stalking and shooting a deer?'

'Of course not,' he said.

'Do you shoot before you've taken aim? No.'

'I think I understand, Snow. Quiet a minute while I try.'

It dint take long for us both to work our way through our checklists perfectly by letting our hands and arms and bodies do the dance, one movement following the next, none out of order.

'Mercies granted,' the hunter said when he'd run through his systems check twice without forgetting anything. 'I thought I'd never get it.'

It weren't long after that Memma announced we'd all passed flying school. The next step would be to practise in a real balloon. But for that to happen we needed to wait for the weather.

Three hawklets

We dint see the hawklets take their first flights but we did begin to see them perched on the walls and roofs of the chateau. I took it to mean that settled weather had arrived. The mother hawk would not have pushed them out of the nest if there was another long storm on the way. So I asked that Gorrie make a start on rebuilding the broken section of wall, and set all other free hands to shovelling snow in the bailey and clearing falls off rooftops. Memma had been consulting her meteorological instruments and declared at the evening meal that we could expect a few days of calm weather.

'I coulda told her that,' the hunter mumbled.

Memma and the mother hawk's forecast held true. The next day was so calm the hunter swore he could hear pine needles dropping in the forest. For others the deep drifts of snow had the odd effect of absorbing sound, so that you found you had to repeat yourself often to be heard, even when standing right by the person you were talking to.

'Or perhaps it's just that people have gone deaf from the screaming gale these last months,' Cook was heard to gripe at a hard-of-hearing dish-hand.

A pause between storms was not time to be wasted. Balloon-flying was delayed until repairs could be made.

Dog-boy did all his tasks in double-quick time, asken for the next one while he was still finishing the one he was on. His good eye flicked between his task and the sky, anxious that we didn't miss this rare flying window. After he finished his work he hurried back to the library to continue with balloon preparation.

Finally the goats were back in their own shed and the surviving chickens had a roof over their heads as well. The break in the wall had been repaired better than new, the fresh mortar still setting, and the cellar ventilation had also been repaired. The bailey was swept clean and broken panes in the glasshouses fixed. There was still the west tower that badly needed work but that would have to wait for now. I announced at our evening meal that if Memma judged the weather favourable then the balloon-testing could go ahead the next day.

Dog-boy and Rose Red jumped up and danced a jig. The hunter and I felt less than jiggy about leaving the safety of solid earth but still there was a flutter in my stomach that I decided to call excitement rather than terror.

The morning was dim and bitingly cold. Dog-boy, jumping out of his skin with excitement, told us that cold air would make it easier to launch the balloons, for the difference between the warm air and cold would add lift.

The baskets were carried out into the bailey which had been cleared of all clutter and freshly swept. Next the silks were rolled out. There was no breeze but they were so light they stirred a little whenever anyone passed by. Memma carried a clipboard with her checklists. Dog-boy would be the first to launch. He'd been looking forward to this moment ever since he'd seen Memma's crash, and he were practically jumping out of his skin. The idea of a flying craft, one that had never entered his head before he saw one, had taken root and bloomed. There he was, dressed in a tan-coloured flying suit just like Memma's. Made of canvas waterproofed with wax, it was also hung about with pockets for storing useful tools and flying instruments. As he settled in his basket, he pulled down his one-eyed goggles, and clipped his cap strap under his chin.

'Commence pre-flight checks,' Memma said, referring to her clipboard.

Dog-boy set to work.

The burner had been stoked and warm air was steadily filling the silk envelope, making it waft and waver like candle smoke. I held my breath because it was unexpectedly beautiful. The quiet crackle of the fire and the rustle of the silk could be heard above the hush of onlookers as they too were caught in the wonder of it. Everyone had gathered for the launch and spirits were high. This was the moment we'd all been working toward for so long. The wonder of flight but now also, the chance to really lift the sky, and not just by coincidence this time. It weren't going to be a matter of singing birds or dead girls coming back to life. This would be science. This would be an expedition backed by research and planning. Still, it were just a theory, as Memma kept reminding us, but it was a theory we were going to test.

Scanning the crowd my eye was drawn to a smaller group, perched on the goat shed roof. It were the three hawklets, Lady, Zephyr and Tyke, watching the show. They were fully fledged now, but their feathers were a lighter grey than their mother's darker brown. They nipped at each other and danced up and down the roofline, looking exactly like the siblings they were.

Soon the balloon silks began to lift and when the envelope cleared the paving and soared upright there was a cheer. Dog-boy, momentarily distracted from the serious business of being a pilot, turned to look up at it, his good eye open in astonishment.

He turned to Rose Red. 'It's working,' he said. 'It's really working!'

Memma, business-like and somewhat immune to the miracle of flying, told him, 'Commence flight check. Thou art free to launch whence thee please, pilot. Setteth thy course and timer and descend anon as thee reacheth the meeting point.'

'Yes, madame,' Dog-boy answered. He began releasing ballast from the bags strapped to the outside of his basket. The basket shifted on the ground, becoming lighter, the balloon tugging at the basket's weight. The basket lifted for a moment, and then settled again. 'Release more ballast, pilot,' Memma said. Dog-boy cautiously released half a bag of weight, and he was away. As he rose, smoothly and slowly, the balloon spun, revealing the sigil Rose had been arguing for on the silks. It was an embroidered image of a dog with an eye-patch, black against the yellow silk of Dog-boy's balloon. It was utterly beautiful and my throat closed over in wonder.

Poke, however, were less impressed, and with a sudden leap he pulled away from my slackened hold on his collar and ran into the empty space under the basket, jumping to try and join his friend in the basket. Dog-boy leaned over the edge. 'Down, boy! Wait there, I'll be back, I promise.'

Poke sat, whining as he watched his friend rise slowly into the sky above.

'Next pilot, commence pre-flight checks,' Memma said. I realised by the lurch in my stomach that I were going next.

I stepped into the basket and took my flying position, trembling all over. The routine of doing my pre-flight checks had the effect of settling my nerves and everything went according to plan so by the time I floated free I was feeling awed and humbled. My silks were dark blue and bore my own sigil, a likeness of Little Bear, of course. Rose Red's was a needle and thread against red silk, and the hunter's balloon was green like the mountain forests and bore his falcon, wings open in full flight. The sigils, apart from making the balloons even more beautiful, would help us tell each craft apart in the sky as the fleet flew.

Memma did not fly with us on our test flight but instead kept a close watch from the east tower through the binocs. One by one we conducted our pre-flight checks and one by one the balloons filled with warm air and floated free of the bailey.

Our first flight went according to plan. Dog-boy even managed to return to the chateau and land in the bailey, just to show off. The rest of us ascended to just below the cloud line, travelled north to the edge of the forest and then descended to land safely in heavy snowfalls. Retrieving parties emerged from the chateau to meet us and the baskets were placed on sleds and pulled back.

The test flight cured almost all of my doubts and fears. Once on the ground, all I wanted was to go up again. I could see the same thrill on the faces of Rose Red and the hunter as we met and embraced, celebrating our return to solid ground.

'The quiet up there!' the hunter said.

'The forest from above looks like a lush green rug,' Rose Red exclaimed. 'I've never seen anything so beautiful.'

I were in agreement. Without knowing it, I'd searched my whole life for the freedom of being aloft in a balloon. Alone but for my fellow pilots, the sky open all around me, the air felt charged, like I were breathing in pure energy.

'Let's do it again,' the hunter said with uncharacteristic enthusiasm.

I laughed with my whole body. A feeling of joy so strong it was almost overwhelming ran through me.

We have to get everyone flying, I thought. *This is a feeling to share.*

'I am well pleased with our test flight today,' Memma told us. 'Some of thee show true promise as aeronauts of skill,' she continued, looking at Dog-boy, who shone with pride. 'So, anon we prepare f'r our expedition to the frozen lake. Thither is weather coming but mine instruments predict settl'd skies in six days from now.'

'Calm weather follows stormy weather, who'd have thought,' the hunter said dryly. I nudged him quiet with my elbow.

Needless to say, we were travelling light. Fuel bricks, which were dense and long-burning, were stacked in the baskets. Enough to get us there and back, according to Dog-boy and the mister's calculations which crawled all over the chalkboards in the library.

'Worse case being, we're walking home,' I said, to no one in particular. 'And that's been done before.'

We would all launch at the same time on our flight to fire-mountain so, the bailey not being large enough for all five balloons, we dragged them outside the chateau walls. Once again, the burners were lit and our gold, red, blue and green silks, along with Memma's grey, slowly filled with warm air.

At Memma's command, we released our ballasts and the fleet was launched.

A system of flags mounted on our baskets let us communicate when the distances were too far, or the wind too high for shouting, and we had bells to toll amid cloud. Once aloft, we saw the sense in flags and bells because it was easy to drift apart in the vast sky.

We left our people far below, waving us off for as long as they could see us. Sending their hopes with us like a flock of finches. My last glimpse of Cook showed her wiping tears away with her sleeve.

With Memma's craft leading, we flew even higher, and this time we were going through the clouds.

My basket lifted from the ground with the wondrous feeling of lightness I was coming to love and I felt calm and focused. But as we ascended higher and higher, the people below us becoming dots, the chateau like a toy house, my attention turned to where we were headed. The clouds above sat thick and heavy, like a feather pillow. Surely the balloons would bounce off and we'd skid along underneath. I knew they were but water droplets, close together, as Memma had explained, but my instincts told me to brace for impact.

I glanced around at the rest of the fleet. Memma slightly higher, Dog-boy in her wake, Rose Red to the left, or to port as we'd been taught to say, the hunter to starboard, and my craft trailing. As we drew closer and closer to the clouding over my panic rose. I couldn't help it. Fear tightened my chest. I was just about to call out for the hunter to stop, to wait for me, when the three hawklets alighted on my basket on silent wings.

I laughed out loud. 'Not getting left behind?' I said, my own voice a comfort. The two brothers, having looked me and my basket over, turned and fell back into open air, their wings catching and lifting immediately. Lady did not follow her brothers and I took it to be a mark of her faith in me. It were a small comfort, but still, as we approached the underside of the clouding over, I wasn't sure what to expect and held my breath.

Above the clouds

>>———→

We did not bounce off the clouds but instead, one by one, we disappeared into them. As we got closer the solid mass of moisture broke up into tendrils, opening to us like wavering fingers. Then it was a heavy mountain mist that gradually drew thicker around us, like the fog that had helped the hunter and me when we were running from Stoat the first time. Memma was enveloped first, and then Dog-boy. My balloon was about level with the hunter's and I gave him the green flag to show all was well. As the mist closed in around us I lost sight of the rest of the fleet, and cloud droplets settled on me and my basket like light rain. Water gathered on my flying suit before rolling off the waxed fabric. I did my checks to calm my nerves, made sure the burner was stoked, trimmed my wings for maximum upward ascent and settled down to wait. Lady, perched on my bow like a captain, shook her wings free of water one by one. She were the expert flyer and I were the novice. As the clouds became thicker and thicker I was grateful for her company. I'd never felt so alone. Not even on the first night in the forest after the hunter left me and before Little Bear found me. At least I'd had the trees then. The clouds did not live or breathe in the same way. They were empty. And so, so silent.

And just then I heard the clang of a bell, three long deep tolls, the signal that Memma had emerged above the clouds, into open sky. I was still whited-in and could not see past the bow of my basket. Even my balloon above was shrouded from view. I looked upward, as if I might catch the moment of climbing up and out of the clouds.

Dog-boy's bell next, three tolls that somehow conveyed his excitement. A few moments later the higher-pitched tolls of Rose Red's bell, and finally the hunter's deliberate three clangs.

I could not see an opening above me. It seemed the clouds were pressing in closer. I started to worry I was stuck somehow, drifting sideways through the cloud layer rather than rising straight up through it. Kicking myself for forgetting to be a pilot, I checked my instruments to see if I was still ascending. They told me I was and I closed my eyes to see if I could feel the balloon rising. When I opened them, I were above the clouds.

For a few long moments I was so overcome I forgot to make my signal but when I did, my bell rang loud through clear skies. The fleet was in perfect formation though I had drifted a little behind. I trimmed my wings to fly slowly closer.

I had some time to look about me then and try to absorb the magic of it. In some ways the top of the clouds were not unlike drifts of snow on solid land, white and softly mounded. But of course, I could not step out of my basket to walk on them, no matter how tempting.

But above! Craning my neck to see, there was nothing overhead but clear sky of the palest blue. The light was empty and bright in a way it never was underneath the clouding over, where we lived in dullness and shadow. And the sun! It was only a pale yellow disc low in the sky ahead of us, and a vast distance away, but still I could feel its warmth through my flying suit. It seemed to penetrate the cold air like a touch. I closed my eyes a moment to feel it but was interrupted once again by Memma's bell.

We flew north, having ascended into an air current that was moving in that direction. These currents were like rivers high in the sky, Memma had taught us. They could be somewhat unpredictable, but generally at lower altitudes they were gentle. The higher you flew the stronger they became. Sometimes, she warned us, we might come across drafts of warmer air sweeping up from the mountains below. These we needed to be careful about as they could push us off course.

On the hour Memma's bell tolled to remind us to make our checks but the rest of the time I were carried off in blissful delight. My basket rocked gently like a cradle and my reclined flying position was like my favourite window seat in the chateau library. It were cold, but not unbearable and unlike on the ground, there was the wondrous, miraculous heat from the sun. I studied the shades of pale blue as the day passed, darker further away from the sun, and lighter the closer I looked until right at the edges where I could only hold my gaze for a second through slitted eyes. The glowing white halo moved across the sky in front of us and to my surprise started sinking down toward the top of the clouds. I kicked myself when I realised that this was the sun setting, as it did every day. I were so used to light appearing and disappearing as it were filtered through the clouding over, I had forgotten that there was actually a big lamp moving across the sky. Two long tolls from Memma's bell signalled we were to begin our descent. We could not fly through the night, she'd decided, it was too dangerous. We would not be able to see each other, and it would also be very cold, which meant the air rivers would become unpredictable. So we would make our way down through the clouding over and find a place to spend the night on solid land.

I opened the port at the very top of my balloon envelope to let some warm air escape, trimmed my wings for descent and immediately felt a dropping in my belly. The top of the clouds loomed up and once again we were enshrouded in thick mist. One by one the fleet emerged underneath the clouding over. This time I were first, and tolled my bell once, the others following not long after me. Below us I could see a vast snowy valley, with silver lines of frozen river running through it. I cracked my teeth together with the jolt of my landing. There was a lot of flying in the last moments as the ground rushed up. Alighting softly would take some more practise.

Once I was back on solid ground Lady landed gracefully on the edge of my basket.

'All right, all right, I got a lot to learn,' I told her. 'You don't have to make a point of it.'

The others, all more skilled flyers than me, managed to land their balloons very near mine and soon we had a fire lit and a meal to warm us. The three hawklets joined us and we shared some of Cook's sausage with them.

We passed a quiet night under Memma's tent. It were further than I'd ever travelled before and though it were strange land, it were not much different from where we'd come from. The hunter and I walked about in the dark and caught two rabbits for our pot before going to sleep. We were alert for the sound of wild bears, without Little Bear to scare them off for us. We needed to hunt whenever we could because our rations were sparse, being only what the balloons could lift. A whole person and fuel was heavy enough, so everything else had to be light.

Before dawn, which I understood now to be when the sun rose in the east, we were preparing for flight again. This would be the day Memma said we'd arrive at the frozen lake, all being well. As our balloons were being warmed we gathered.

'The weather is favourable,' she began. 'But thither is a storm approaching on the morrow. If we see any sign of it we shall descend immediately. Ye understand, pilots?' We all nodded. 'Anon, we shall ascend to the north airstream and sail north-east as planned. Recall thy training closely, pilots. Stayeth in tight formation. And bell signals on the hour, flags on the half-hour, prithee.'

Our launch and ascent went smoothly. We left the unfamiliar valley with its frozen rivers and tame rabbits and sailed up through the clouding over, once again entering the gentle flow of the air river. Lady joined me. She'd caught a mouse for breakfast and started ripping it apart with her sharp talons. I looked away in disgust, telling her she needed to learn some table manners if she were going to eat in company.

We flew through the day, keeping close together in our diamond formation, doing our checks and setting our flags. The sun climbed up and across the sky in front of us in a gentle arc. It were like an old friend now, one that gave warm hugs and were always happy to see you.

That day we were joined by the sun's sister, the moon. A pale wedge of grey river pebble, crossing the sky on her own arc, but shy and cold and slipping away below the cloud horizon before the day was well underway. I tried not to be distracted by the comings and goings of these wondrous things because I had the business of flying to attend to, and because as the sun began its descent we were approaching the part of our journey that required some skilled piloting.

We needed to navigate our way to the frozen lake, avoiding the jagged edges of the crater it lay in. It were important to be precise in our landing, otherwise we'd have to carry the baskets overland which would be laborious and time-consuming. However, all Memma's navigating was done while we were blind to solid land. It would be only her instruments and her skilled reading of them that would tell us when we were close, and then we'd descend, hopefully without crashing into the side of a mountain. That would be the thorny part.

Memma hung out her flag to signal to standby and the warm-air balloon pilots trimmed our wings to hold steady. From my position at the back I couldn't see what Memma was doing in her basket. I hung over the edge, my basket rocking in protest as the wings resisted the flow of the air. It were like dipping your hand in a fast-flowing river and feeling the push of the water. The balloons wanted to fly and holding them back made them buck and sway like restless horses. Finally Memma gave the port-trim signal flag and we followed her on that heading.

Glancing toward the hunter, I saw him waving and pointing behind us. Instead of the endless field of undulating white cloud-tops, there was a looming mass of black turbulence. Frothing and foaming like river rapids, the grey-black and menacing clouds were gaining on us. My belly turned to lead. Memma's bell tolled for a course change and I applied my mind to flying, noticing my hands were shaking.

Just then Lady gave a call in her raspy young bird-voice.

Looking up from my piloting I saw another grey cloud ahead of us, but this one rose up through the puffy white clouding over and was shaped like a deathcap mushroom. It was the eruption from fire-mountain, I realised. The cause of the clouding over, and it were plain to see why now. Dead ahead was a maelstrom of surging smoke and ash, tumbling over itself in a constant rolling motion. Occasionally, fiery spouts surged up through the middle of the mushroom, falling back into the black smoke and disappearing from sight. My heart thudded painfully in my chest and my hands shook even more.

We were losing light and being squeezed between a storm and a volcano. Below were more mountain volcanos, smaller and some with huge craters in their tops, filled with solid or liquid, who knew? All of a sudden it struck me what a folly this was. Filling a silk balloon with warm air and hanging a basket underneath by some rope with nothing below but empty air. Falling all that way to the ground would be the slowest and fastest trip a person could make at the same time. My throat closed over and my mouth went dry. I could feel my heart racing. I couldn't work out which threat was worse, the storm or fire-mountain. Where was there to run? My vision seemed to narrow and blacken at the edges.

This was panic. And it were no time to lose my head. I took a moment to close my eyes and feel the cold air on my skin.

Remember your training, Snow, I told myself firm. *One step at a time, like always. Flying is just like climbing a mountain, losing your head in a panic is certain death.* I looked to Memma's flags and trimmed my wings to follow.

The frozen lake

We swooped and banked in our descent. Memma's direction flags came quickly, one after the other. My hands were so busy trimming the wings and releasing the balloon's vent control line I no longer had time to be terrified, I just needed to keep up. We were chasing the sun as it sank. The clouds raced up to meet us and we passed through them, this time maintaining our course, rather than sinking like a fresh egg in a bucket of water. Wind streamed through my wings. My full attention was on listening for Memma's bells. We were to maintain whatever course we were on as we passed through the cloud layer while we couldn't see Memma's flags to guide us. This meant a few minutes of holding our nerve and hoping we weren't about to slam into the side of a mountain. Those minutes passed quickly, travelling as fast as we were. When we emerged, my balloon only moments after the others', we heard Memma's single toll. I looked to her flags for our next heading and adjusted my wings. It were only then that I had a moment to look about me.

Lady, having ridden with me through the clouds, launched and soared on her wide wings beneath my basket, taking in the scene below. As far as I could see were the ragged tops of the volcanic mountains. It were a field of smoky, fiery belching and burping, like the miners at their pipes after dinner. The bare earth was black and strewn with sharp rocks and the telltale rounded streams of rock that had once flowed in molten rivers. In my life I'd seen rivers of water, rivers of air and now here were rivers of rock. Patches of lush green vegetation grew on the warm mountainsides where snow melted quickly. But there were also fields of glacier clinging to steep rock faces and stuck in crevices. Here and there holes in the ground were filled with steaming bubbling mud. It was a strange land of steam and snow rubbing elbows like awkward cousins.

Memma's navigating had not crashed us into a mountainside, but we still had quite a way to descend, and the black storm clouds were now eating the remaining light of the day. The wind was becoming stronger, my balloon flexing and flapping. I stoked my burner to keep the silk taut but at the same time I needed to slowly release warm air through the parachute flap to descend. I worked hard, peering through the gathering gloom to see Memma's flags and following her directions diligently. It would be a close thing to land before the storm closed in on us.

At that moment I noticed the hunter's green balloon caving in, his falcon sigil creased in the middle, a sign the air inside was cooling rapidly and not holding tight against the wind. I trimmed my wings to sail closer and saw that he was struggling to light his burner. A gust of wind must have blown it out. He hadn't tolled his bell yet, it were three short clangs for an emergency, but his descent was steeper than the rest of the fleet's. Already the ground was rushing up and I placed a hand on my bell to signal the emergency. At the last moment I saw a dim flame light and the hunter closed his burner and looked to trim his wings.

Memma had noticed the deviation, and put out flags for a change of course so the fleet stayed close to the hunter's balloon. This brought us around the edge of a green-sided volcano and then the frozen lake was in view. The storm was bringing sheets of rain, so we could only see part of it clearly but it was vast, and perfectly smooth, like a polished mirror. Memma changed our course one last time. We were to land on the hard, glassy surface of the lake, close to the dam that had formed at its valley head. The hunter's balloon was still descending too fast, the burner not having had time to re-heat the air inside his balloon. Even with his parachute flap closed, it was going to be a heavy landing, but hopefully not a crash.

I could not watch, though I wanted to, because I needed to avoid my own hard landing. Memma and Dog-boy alighted on the lake surface at about the same moment, light as feathers. Rose Red too made an elegant descent, in spite of the strong winds rocking her basket. The hunter, at the last moment, changed course and headed for a drift of snow at the edge of the lake, a short distance away. It were a wise decision as a strong gust of wind knocked his basket over and sent the hunter tumbling into the snow bank.

My landing, mercies granted, was my best yet. I had barely touched down and doused my burner before I were running to see whether he was hurt. The others got there first and had him sitting up. He'd bitten a hole in his lip which were already swollen.

'I'm or'right, Snow,' he told me as I threw my arms around

him. 'But ouch, I might've cracked a rib now you're squeezing me like that.'

'Are you sure?' I asked, patting him all over to feel for broken bones.

'I'm fine,' he said again, smiling. 'Not my most graceful landing, but safe on solid ground now.'

'Not f'r long,' Memma said, eyeing the storm that was upon us, the wind whipping around, and heavy snow starting to fall. 'We're going to needeth one of thy shelters f'r the night, hunter. The silks shall not standeth this.'

'Short notice, madame,' the hunter said. 'But let's see what can be done.'

Working quickly, we dragged the baskets together and tied and pegged them firmly to the ice. It was slippery work, sliding all over the glassy surface in our boots.

Then we followed the hunter to find shelter. We went for the lee side of the crater and climbed a way up before we found a crevice with an overhang. Not quite a cave, but it were out of the wind and we could make a fire and stay warm while the storm passed over.

As they always do, I thought. *Just a matter of how long.*

The drowned city

←——≪

With nothing to do while waiting out the storm, Dog-boy asked Memma to explain again why we had come to fire-mountain.

According to the scientists of the Restoration, Memma's civilisation across the sea, fire-mountain was spewing a mixture of gas and ash high into the atmosphere. Over time this had formed a layer in the sky that started reflecting the sun back into space. Underneath, the world became cold. She called this a volcanic winter and explained that over generations, cold makes more cold. Frozen rivers become glaciers, seasonal sea-ice freezes permanently.

The hunter grunted in agreement. If there's one thing we understood, it was the cold.

What we were about to attempt would break the cold cycle and let the sun in.

When the frozen water held in the lake melted and started to flow down the valley, it would seep into the sides of the volcano and cool the fire within. Like Cook said, throwing water on a fire makes steam and there would be plenty of that, according to Memma, but eventually the water of the melted lake would quell the ferocity of fire-mountain and in time the sun would burn away the clouding over.

'It's true the cold is becoming colder,' the hunter said. 'And ifen the long nights get any longer and darker, it won't be possible to wait them out behind our stone walls. People are like plants, we need light to live. We already got clouded over and snowed in, and once every drop of liquid water is frozen, that's it for us.'

'Hence the needeth to save ourselves,' Memma said.

The hunter frowned, struggling to find the words. 'From what I heard,' he began, 'folk in the past had a tendency to get ahead of themselves. And in my experience nature has a way of reminding us to mind how much we think of ourselves.'

'You mean if we put out the volcano we might somehow make the cold worse?' asked Dog-boy sceptically.

'We don't know, that's my point.'

'The science suggests . . .' Memma began.

'I got a lot of respect for your instruments and measurements, Memma. It's just that some things can't be known by measuring.'

'Some things you have to know by feeling,' I finished for him.

'Ifen we don't remember our place, the mountain'll find a way to do it for us. And we are flesh and blood, not rock and fire.'

'No one will get hurt, hunter,' Memma said. 'I'll make sure of that.'

'Meaning no disrespect, madame,' the hunter replied mildly, 'but that's exactly the kind of thinking that led to the trouble in the first place.'

When the storm passed I walked up the side of the crater a ways to rest on a patch of green grass, sweeping my hand over the lush growth for the novelty of it. Lady landed by me. She were never far away on the mountain and I liked her company. She climbed on my forearm, her sharp young talons digging into my skin.

'You can do that now,' I told her. 'But when you're grown you'll need to clip your toenails, bird.'

She ducked her head and let me stroke her soft feathers. She were quiet for a moment, and walked up my arm to perch on my shoulder, spending a minute grooming my hair like she did her own feathers, getting it to lay down flat, pulling some out by the roots.

'Ow!' I told her, but she paused just then and lifted her head, looking toward the middle of the lake. I followed her gaze and noticed a reflection, something glinting gold under the surface.

The hunter, walking down the slope and stopping behind me, had seen it too. 'Let's have a look,' he said.

Rose Red was the most adept among us at gliding on the ice in her boots. I was slowly getting a feeling for the push-slide action but my backside was black and blue from falling over. For once Dog-boy was the worst at something. Rose Red gave him her arm and he gratefully accepted.

The hunter and I proceeded cautiously on our own as holding onto each other tended to bring us both down. Memma's healed ankle was not up the strain of skating so she kneeled on a piece of thick folded cloth and pushed herself over the ice with gloved hands, making the easiest way of all of us.

We skated toward the middle of the lake. Above us were the edges of the great crater, weathered to smooth ridges. The lake was almost perfectly round, an uncanny shape for a lake, I thought. A river was a ribbon and a mountain creviced and cracked and weathered in every direction. A pebble were rarely round but more often flattened and oval. But the lake was as round as a bubble before it bursts.

Coming up closer to the glinting gold that had turned into a shimmering haze, hanging low over the surface of the lake, we stared in disbelief. Beneath our feet was a city trapped under ice.

Memma said, 'It hast flooded whence the volcano erupted and all the glaciers on the mountain melted.'

'Must've happened slowly, otherwise everything would be washed away,' Dog-boy added.

The frozen water of the lake was miraculously clear so the whole sunken city was visible under the ice. And it was beautiful. There were domed roofs tiled in intricate patterns, neatly paved streets, open-air baths and even gardens still green and frozen in place. As we skated over the rooftops we had the same view as a bird, or a balloon, hovering in the sky. Every detail was perfectly preserved. We came to a halt when we reached the centre of the city where there was a giant round paved area tiled with an intricate mosaic depicting people and mountains and rivers and a huge volcano. The five of us stood staring at it, lost for words.

Slowly I started to realise it was a story told in pictures. It showed people growing crops and having babies and weaving cloth. There were markets and festivals and dignitaries wearing robes. In one sequence a battle was fought, the soldiers wearing helmets and swinging long daggers in close fighting. All of these stories began in the northern corner, in front of a huge domed structure that reminded me a little of the council office in Fox's city, and continued in a circle all the way around, like telling the time on a clockface. At the centre was fire-mountain. In the mosaic the volcano looked demure and calm. Smoke wafted from its crater and snow dusted its peak. It was a strong contrast to the charred and fiery mountain we were standing below now.

Dog-boy dropped to his knees and pointed at the top of picture. 'It starts there,' he said.

'How do you know?' asked Rose Red.

Dog-boy looked sheepish. 'I like stories. I can find them anywhere.'

'High in the hot ash mountains, there is a golden city hidden in an ancient lake bed. It is full of stone buildings carved with mythical creatures and gardens bursting with life. The people who live there are gifted gardeners. There is nowhere in the city that isn't covered with climbing vines, flowers in bloom and shade trees to rest beneath. The air is filled with bees and butterflies.

'For many years the seasons of life turn without interruption; harvests, feasts, games, weddings, funerals. The city lives in the shadow of the fire-mountain which sometimes rumbles and shakes but also gifts them fertile ash and soil that makes their gardens grow lush and green.

'One day the volcano belches and a child is hurt by a flying rock. Look there, he's made lame. You can see his crutches. The fire-mountain god, see him? He uses the volcano's heat to forge his weapons. He carries a hammer and an axe and sometimes he stokes his blacksmithing fires too hot. He feels sorry for hurting the boy and so he forges some coins, throwing them into the town square where they sink to the bottom of a clear fountain. The god tells the boy that if the city is ever threatened by the volcano, the coins will cool its fires. Sure enough, when the god next carelessly stokes his fires too hot, the volcano roars and rains ash and rocks on the city. The glaciers begin to weep water, slowly flooding the streets of the city. So the boy climbs the mountain. Even though he becomes caked in ash, he struggles to the top and throws in one of the coins. At once the mountain quietens and cools. Life in the city returns to normal. From then on the fountain's treasure of coins is closely guarded. See the dragon statue coiled around it?'

He paused, catching his breath.

'Wait,' Dog-boy said, noticing a new sequence of pictures. 'There's more. An army appears, marching over the mountain to ransack the city. The coins are stolen. Look, there they go, in a treasure chest onboard a ship sailing away across an ocean.'

'So the next time the volcano erupted, there were no magic coins to cool its fires and the city was flooded and the clouding-over closed in,' Rose Red finished.

We had all been following the story as Dog-boy pointed it out under the ice. We looked at each other now, stunned and saddened.

'It's just a story,' I said. 'One to tell children before bed.'

Memma was kneeling on the ice, peering at the magical golden coins, trying to get a closer look.

I followed her gaze. I saw what she saw. It were true they looked like the fire-mountain coins I'd taken from my dead mother's tomb. The same ones we were using for her catalyst, only now, with the passage of time, they had turned black and thick with tarnish.

Memma sat back on her heels and turned her sharp gaze on me. It made me uncomfortable. I said again, 'It's just a story. Dog-boy told it well. Too well, perhaps. But still, only a story.'

'I don't get it,' Rose Red said. 'You can't see the picture from on the ground. You have to be up high. So who's it for?'

The hunter glanced over his shoulder to where the volcano steamed and hissed and fumed behind us. 'It's for us. It's a warning.'

The god of fire-mountain

>⟶

We returned to our camp in the dark, in silence. The discovery of the city, and all the people who must have been lost when it was flooded, had made us feel small and sorry. As we sat quietly around our fire I gazed up at fire-mountain. There was a glow at its peak from the fires burning within. As I watched it seemed to brighten and dim like a heartbeat. Occasionally flares would fly up into the sky, like Cook's stove throwing sparks when it were stirred. Except fire-mountain sparks were more likely to be the size of boulders. We went to our beds deep in thought.

In the morning there was work to do and we put the sunken city out of our minds. We had to re-make our balloons into a giant silk dome. Rose Red had devised the pattern for this transformation and worked on the picking and stitching until the tips of her fingers were raw. Soon the dome took shape, laid out on the lake. Climbing up the crater-side one evening to see our work, and that of the silk worms, to give the creatures their due credit, took my breath away. Each section, grey, red, dark blue, gold and green seemed lit from underneath by the glow of the lake. Our sigils, Poke, Little Bear, the falcon and the needle, were linked together in this great cause.

And then it was back to work. I were sitting on the frozen ground, my backside numb, swearing over pricking my fingers with my needle and struggling to keep up with my share of the sewing work, when Lady made a long call. The hunter and I both glanced up to where she hovered in the sky above us. It were not one of her usual calls, those to her brothers, who were also around but dint like to come close to human company, or sometimes those she made when she'd caught a mouse, kind of a singing then. This call were an alert and the hunter and I put down our needles. We'd barely reached the crest of the crater when I were bowled over by a great mass of dark-brown fur.

I had time to think, *This is it. I been killed by a bear finally.* But then I realised I were being licked to death, not ripped to shreds. It were Little Bear, and right behind her, now bounding down the hill toward Dog-boy, Poke.

I couldn't believe my eyes. 'You walked all this way, Little Bear? To find us?'

My bear sat on her backside and raised her nose in the air to say, *You think you were going to leave us behind? Think again, Snow.*

There were cries of joy, both boy and barking, coming from down on the lake as Dog-boy and Poke rolled around together. The hunter and I grinned at each other.

'Extra mouths to feed,' I told him.

'Int that what a family is?' he replied with a wry smile.

Lady called again from where she hung in the sky above, as if to remind us that she wasn't going anywhere either.

Little Bear turned then, like she were going back for something she'd forgotten. Then we saw that she had a cub. A little bear of her own. My eyes filled with tears at the sight. It were a boy, by the looks, and very young, just a pēpē, probably born along the way. Little Bear nudged him forward with her long snout and he approached me cautiously, baby whiskers twitching. I held out my hand and finally he found the courage to lick me, dog-like, with his soft velvet tongue.

'Well done, Little Bear,' I told her, digging my fingers into my bear's scruff. 'He's a precious baby.'

'Is that what we'll call him then?' asked the hunter. 'Baby bear?'

I laughed.

Nothen made me happier than having my bear close by.

But no sooner were we reunited than the ground started to tremble beneath us.

PART III

Snow climbs

>>———→

The earthquake was the first sign. Soon after the ground turned to jelly we knew the volcano was angry again. This wasn't hard to know because it seemed the sky began raining down on us. Hot ash and small pebbles pelted the lake, making it hiss and steam. We were all knocked off our feet, Poke letting out a yelp of alarm.

'Make haste, gather the silks!' called Memma.

If they were burned we would never make it home, so we scrambled, all of us in a mad rush, to pull in the dome and squash it into the baskets, sliding them across the lake to the shelter of our rock crevice as quickly as we could. All the while, hot ash fell. It stung our bare skin and burned our throats as we worked. Copying Rose Red, I wound my scarf around my face until I could only see through a slit. When the silks were bundled and the baskets were banked up under snow we raced for shelter.

It were a terrifying few hours. The ground shook and the sky were first lit up with a fiery glow and then blanketed by thick black rolls of smoke and steam rushing down the sides of fire-mountain. We huddled together, people and animals, our backs to the worst of it, holding each other and sayen over and over, *Let it be done soon*. It were worse than waiting out even the strongest blizzard. This was the ground underneath us trying to toss us away, to throw us off the very earth.

At last the ground stopped shivering and with the light of day, the volcano did not seem as frightening. We emerged from our rock crevice that was not quite a cave and brushed the thick coating of ash off of each other's clothing. I laughed in spite of how frightened I was when I saw the hunter. Under his scarf his face was completely black with soot, the whites of his eyes glowing.

'If you're laughing at me, Little Queen, you should remember you look just the same,' he told me.

Below us the lake lay in shards, like a dropped mirror on cold tiles. 'I wonder what's happened to the hidden city,' Dog-boy said.

Memma had been quiet but she spoke up now. 'The mountain must be appeased.'

The rest of us stopped what we were doing and looked at her.

'Just like in the story? Aren't you a scientist, madame? I thought scientists dint believe in gods, or magic coins, or whatever it is,' the hunter said.

Memma turned her sharp chin toward him. 'All things canst be explained by the science we know, sir. There is much yet to be explain'd. The last thing we needeth is f'r the volcano to becometh fierce again. If 'tis quiet at the hour the wat'r of the lake is released the fire shall wend out quietly. If 'tis burning bright, then the wat'r may not be'est enough to put out the fires that burneth within. Acc'rding to the legend und'r the ice, the ancient people believed the mountain is liketh a living

148

thing. It can be'est appealed to and appeased. So someone must wend up the mountain.'

I remembered that part of the story. The robes boy with the bad leg covered in ash, trudging up the side of the volcano, holding a coin.

Memma continued. 'It should be Snow who goes. The coins belong to her, mayhap the mountain will listen when she speaketh.'

'The mountain is like a god?' the hunter asked. 'Or at least, that's what those people believed?'

'A deity yond fills the sky with its roar and makes the ground tremble und'r its feet. That is the legend,' Memma said.

'And it can be calmed with a fire-mountain coin? Just like in the picture?' Dog-boy said.

Memma tilted her head in reply. 'Mayhap. There could be'est some truth in the magical coin. We know 'tis a pow'rful catalyst f'r flying. Perchance it can also quiet a volcano. Many things are beyond our understanding, sir.'

The hunter turned to me. I stood there with my mouth hanging open. I couldn't believe this were happening. I looked at him, placing my hands on my hips. 'Now, hold on, you're not believing her, are you?'

The hunter shrugged. 'How would Snow appease the mountain-god? Just like she can talk to trees and bears?' he asked Memma.

I turned to Little Bear crossly. 'This is your fault,' I told her. 'Soon as you turn up, people lose their minds.'

Her reply was a yawn, showing her sharp white teeth, all the way to the back of her head. *All I did was come and find you,* she was saying.

'Just the same as in the myth,' Memma replied.

'Are you serious?' I asked her. 'I int climbing a volcano while it's spewing fire. What in heck do I know about mountain gods?' I looked to the hunter, to see if he could talk some sense into her.

To my alarm he had a look I'd seen before, a long time ago. The one he got when he first saw me having a conversation with Little Bear.

'How'd she find us up here, Snow?' he asked, waving toward my bear. 'We flew through the air, it's not like she could follow our scent trail. There's something uncanny in how you speak to creatures, and maybe it'll work on volcanos as well.'

'Likely you'll have to sing to it, miss. Do you know any songs?' Dog-boy added dryly.

I couldn't believe it. Lady chose that moment to swoop out of the sky and land on my shoulder.

The hunter raised his hands palm up as if to say, *See?*

So it was decided I would do the same as the boy in the story.

'Do I have to bow and sing a song, as well as toss the coin in?' I complained.

'Do whatever you believe will appease the mountain,' Memma said.

This dint sit well with me at all. 'That's perfect,' I grumbled. 'Why's it have to be me? Int my fault I got a bear. I killed her mother, who else were going to look after her?'

'*I* killed her mother,' the hunter reminded me. 'Don't you think there's a chance the story is true and the volcano is living in some strange way? Do you not yourself talk to trees?'

'It int talking, exactly,' I said stubbornly. 'Not using words.'

'Then don't use words when you talk to the volcano,' the hunter said. 'Do like you do with trees.'

It just made me crosser that the hunter reminded me of these things that dint make any sense to me. In my opinion anyone could do the same if they put their minds to it.

'All right,' I said, without any good grace at all. 'I'll go.'

Rose Red hugged me even though I were being horrible.

The climb would not be without its hazards. I had to cover myself from head to toe against falling debris. Convincing Little Bear to wear boots over her paws took some doing but eventually I talked her into not chewing them off.

The hunter said the baby bear would have to come with us. 'He goes where Little Bear goes and she follows you,' he said.

But I were firmly against him coming and told the hunter he'd have to hold onto him no matter how much he cried after us.

Poke would stay with Dog-boy but no doubt Lady would join the climbing party. I were grateful she at least could look after herself. In fact I wished I could grow wings and fly instead of having to climb.

Memma advised I make the trip as quickly as I could. She explained the gases close to the volcano crater would be poisonous to breathe and the ground would be very hot.

'Anything else?' I said, still cranky. 'Climbing a volcano to toss a coin in without breathing or touching the ground int enough to ask?'

I were feeling a burdensome weight of expectation, and behaving badly. I stomped out of camp, disregarding my friends' well-wishes and hardening my heart to the cub's crying. Cook would have scolded me, possibly even using her wooden spoon for emphasis. And I felt sorry as soon as my feet hit the side of the crater. Once I were putting one foot in front of the other, Little Bear at my side, I started to feel like myself again. My bad temper ebbed away. But it were too late to rush back and say my sorries.

I'll say them when I get back, I told myself. And that would be soon because this were a task to get done quick and proper.

I put on my flying goggles to protect my eyes, wrapped my thick scarf tightly around my face and set a brisk pace, feeling my legs stretch and warm with the walk. I only allowed myself one glance over my shoulder but it were a mistake for when I reached the top of the crater I saw my friends still watching my ascent. I dint pause any longer.

As we climbed I made a plan. I would climb this mountain as if it were any other. I knew how to do that.

We followed snowfalls as much as we could to avoid hot ash, and followed an old path, for I weren't the first to make this ascent. Others had climbed the volcano, but not for some time. I carried one of my mother's coins. I knew it now to be stolen and I felt it weighed down my pack.

As we ascended the mountain the ground became warm in places and patterned with many shades of colours I'd never seen before. At home our mountains were snow-white and brown and green and hardly ever showed yellows or reds except on lichen-covered rocks. And blue was a colour that we almost never saw outside, except for sometimes in a bird's feather or a gleam on an insect wing. It were there in the dyes of our thread and our memories of the sky but on the volcano it appeared more vividly than my eyes could take in. Crusts of cobalt blue and indigo-stained soils coated the ground and we crunched through cautiously, making our way between islands of snow.

Here and there bubbling pools of mud threatened to splatter us if we came too close. It were not country that talked to me. The heated ground made my feet burn inside my boots and I sweated under my clothes. I'd been cold my whole life and this heat dint feel comfortable. Little Bear complained in her own way, shaking herself free of the fine ash often, and rolling in snow when we came to patches that were big enough.

It would be a day's walk up, an uncomfortable camp on the side of the volcano for the night, and a walk down at first light. *The faster the better*, I told myself as we pushed on.

The higher we went the more the landscape changed. The snow patches thinned out, the ground beneath our feet grew warmer and warmer and a steady rain of ash began to fall. It were like snow as it fell softly out of the clouds but when it landed, it was hot rather than cold. Little Bear's coat singed and the smell of burnt fur followed us. But that weren't the worst bad smell coming off the mountain. The air smelled like rotten eggs and hot metal. A taste gathered in my mouth like I'd been sucking a rusty spoon. Memma had told us that the smell was an element called sulphur, an acid that filled the air and would burn most anything it touched.

The path turned to more of a climb and I turned my attention to placing my feet carefully and finding hand-holds. Little Bear made her way like a goat, leaping from one outcrop to the next. Ropes had been placed in the steepest sections though I hesitated to trust them as they were frayed and sometimes broken from the acid air.

Holes began to appear in my clothing and I was glad I were swathed in many layers, even though I were sweating through them. I breathed heavily through the layers of scarf across my face, and my throat was beginning to feel raw. I pulled down the cloth to take a few mouthfuls of lake water from a bottle I carried, warm now though it had been near frozen when I'd collected it. Little Bear licked snow from a crevice she found. Looking up, I saw the edge, finally. It was a mountain without a top, having blown it off like a pot come to rapid boil. I decided I liked my mountains to have peaks, though they were sharp and cold. Anything but the fiery abyss I was heading toward.

I shaded my eyes for the heat was drying them out and called to Little Bear. 'We have to press on. We're almost there.'

A stream of smoke and ash poured upward from the crater into the mushroom-shaped cloud we'd seen from our balloons, even bigger now. I approached bent over, half-turned away. The windy heat and hot gases were overwhelming. Looking to Little Bear I saw that she were coated all over with grey ash, like a statue. She'd given up shaking herself and looked at me accusingly. *You dragged me all the way up here, Snow, now what?*

I pulled the fire-mountain coin from my pack with my awkwardly wrapped hands and held it a moment, looking at the picture of the volcano stamped in the cold hard metal that had once been gold perhaps. Then I tossed it over the edge of the crater into the tremendous updraft of gases. It immediately disappeared. I approached the precipice, coming as close as I could, shielding my face but still feeling my skin grow red and burnt. *Quiet now, fire-mountain*, I told it in my head. *Quiet now and let the sky open again.*

It weren't at all like dropping a stone in a well. The coin might have been vaporised instantly for all I could tell. I retreated and tried to listen again, but there were just volcano sounds coming from the mountain. Nothing that made any sense to me.

My head was spinning.

'What am I supposed to say, Little Bear?' I said aloud. My voice was hoarse and scratchy, the air too nasty to breathe. 'Does the mountain speak to you?'

But she dint answer. She'd curled into a ball and tucked her head away, the only sensible thing to do. I wished I could do the same but I were supposed to be talking to a god. *How'm I supposed to do that?* I wondered again, dropping to my knees on the sharp ground. I closed my eyes to rest them from the intensity of the volcanic cloud. I thought about how the forest used to whisper over me and longed for the cool green shade under those trees. Trees were gossipy beings, always passing stories among themselves, letting each other know what was happening and who was passing from one day to the next. The way I spoke with Little Bear was by watching her ears and whiskers. All her thoughts were there to see.

What did a volcano sound like? Like rumbling and shrieking, like Cook's kettle at full boil, like the hot hiss of the kitchen stove sitting on the cold tiles of the chateau. Like a thick soup bubbling in a pot.

But these were only sounds; if the volcano were speaking to me, I couldn't understand it.

Dark was falling. We'd stayed as long as we could. Calling to Little Bear I turned to find the head of the path and we retreated. We found an icy crevice and squeezed in there to rest. I laid my cheek against cool rock and dozed off.

While I slept I dreamed of a great wave. Its crest rose as high as a mountain and when it broke it washed everything away in roiling whitewater. Forests were uprooted and boulders tossed around like pebbles. Even birds were caught by sucking downdrafts as the water poured through valleys and filled the great high plateaus, turning them into muddy lakes filled with debris.

My loved ones were pulled from my grasp by the rushing currents and lost. As the water covered my own head I panicked and woke with a jump. I opened my eyes to the dim light of a new day, my cheek still pressed to the rock, Little Bear curled up by me. I crawled out of the crevice and looked up toward the erupting peak of fire-mountain, half expecting to see it transformed into a towering wave. It were true the mushroom cloud did resemble frothing whitewater, reaching up to the heavens like water at full boil. I shook myself from sleep, wishing the nightmare away.

We were descending that day. I dint feel I'd spoken to any gods as I'd been asked to, but I were ready to face Memma and tell her we'd done our best. The dream having pulled my family away from me, I were anxious to get back to them to say my sorries. I realised that if someone had to climb the mountain and listen to the volcano then I'd rather it'd been me than any of my friends. I dint know why I'd been so blind to that. I wouldn't have let Dog-boy or Rose Red make the climb. This was no task for even the hunter, who I'd followed up every mountain on the island.

'C'mon, Little Bear. We're going home.'

The Little Queen

>>———>

It weren't a dignified homecoming. Little Bear and I staggered more'n walked back onto the shattered lake. My lungs were raw and burning and my skin was red and irritated where the ash and gas had burned through all the thick layers of my clothing. My bear were singed all over and coughing. First thing she did was find a thick drift of snow and roll in it, throwing up clouds of steam. When she were done with that, she jumped in a special bath Rose Red had made for her, swimming and wallowing and then hauling herself out and giving herself a shake that soaked all of us. It were only after this that the hunter let the baby bear run to her. I saw scratches all over the hunter's arms from the cub's ferocious struggling to follow his mother, and felt guilty all over again for how I'd behaved before I climbed the mountain.

Rose Red and Memma unwound my clothing and helped me into a cool bath that washed away the poisons and soothed my burns.

'The mountain is quieter now,' the hunter said.

I frowned at him. I felt like a fraud because I dint ask anything, or make any agreements with this volcano. All I did was get burned feet and singed hair climbing a nasty hot mountain.

Later I told him, 'It weren't anything I did.'

He just looked at me. Clear and steady.

'Mine own instruments showeth a significant decrease in the seismic activity of the volcano,' Memma said.

'I did nothing, I swear on Little Bear's life,' I told them. 'She curled up in a ball and I tossed a coin in the smoke, like a child making a wish in a well. I dint hear the mountain – or a god – sayen anything.'

'But it seems like it heard you,' was the hunter's irritating reply.

I remembered my dream but I didn't mention it. Sometimes speaking a dream makes it more real, not less, and this felt like one of those. Mercies granted, it could all be forgotten because there was work to be done.

The balloon dome, showing all our sigils and lit from within by the glowing lake and the burners, were a beautiful sight once it were up again. I felt that if the mountain did have eyes to see, it couldn't help but be impressed. But I were trying to forget about gods.

We soon had warm air trapped in the balloon dome. The surface of the lake slowly started to turn to sloshy soft ice. The hunter and I watched the mountain and the weather anxiously and Memma watched her instruments. If a storm came in before we got a good melt happening, the drop in temperature would re-freeze the water and we'd have to start all over again. In that case there wouldn't be enough fuel left. It had to work the first time.

Memma refused when we suggested she hold back enough

catalyst for her journey home. She told us no, that everything depended on this working and we needed every scrap of power from her elixir machine. She said it would be a close thing as it was without holding anything back. I gave her what were left of my fire-mountain coins, pushing them into her hands.

Day by day the ice of the dam melted away. It were thrilling when one morning the trickle turned to a stream and we danced under the tiny waterfall that was beginning to form from the lake edge into the ancient valley below. It turned to a damp dribble as it hit the frozen rocky ground, but it were a start worth celebrating.

But I dreamed of the great wave again. It swept across the island, drowning the forests and pulling the hunter from my arms. In this dream Lady sat perched on my shoulder and whispered in my ear.

The wave, don't you see? The lake melt begins a melt across every snow-topped peak, every glacier.

I suddenly saw what she was tryen to tell me.

'The mountain speaks in dreams,' I said aloud, waking myself up.

There would be a great wave. The vision hit me like a donkey kick in my guts. I saw that once we melted this lake, all the others would follow. This lake would melt the next one and the next one all the way across the island and then to the sea. Once the sea melted we'd be flooded all over again and this time, there wasn't enough land left to sink. The mountain had spoken to me after all, I'd just been too stubborn to hear.

I rushed to Memma to tell her we were making a mistake. She was copying measurements into her logbook. Dog-boy was spooning his dinner to his mouth nearby.

'The island will be flooded. When all the lakes and glaciers are melted, we'll be washed away in a great wave,' I told her, out of breath. 'The mountain spoke to me in a dream.'

Memma looked up at me sharply and spoke to me like I were a child. 'You are but a small island here, Snow. The rest of the world needs the sun. This is a plan f'r the valour of many, not just the few backward folks in this land.' When she spoke her wide blue eyes seemed suddenly cold. ''T'were decided long ago, and not by thee.'

I was stung by her words. 'This was your plan all along?'

'Not exactly. I wast collecting data, but I wast equip'd with orders from the king to doth what I wilt, as mine circumstances evolv'd.'

I turned to Dog-boy. 'Did you know?'

'No,' he said firmly. 'I dint know there were orders from a king.'

Memma turned her gaze on Dog-boy and he became unsure of himself. 'But it doesn't change anything, miss,' he said, though his face was lined with disappointment. 'Still we're going to lift the clouds and for the good of all.'

'That's right, young sir. Thee didst everything expected of thee perfectly.'

Dog-boy frowned and dropped his spoon and bowl with a clatter. 'I dint know there'd be a great wave, madame. I dint know the whole island would be drowned. I dint know any of that until just now.' His eye hardened.

'Calm yourself, young sir,' Memma said, less sure of herself now. ''Tis of nay consequence. By then we will be well away. You and me will survey the whole globe. There are many more dis'covries to be made. Thou wilt be mine apprentice.'

The hunter and Rose Red entered camp.

'What's going on?' the hunter asked, seeing my face.

'Dog-boy, what's wrong?' Rose said, going to his side.

My throat was closing over in shock and I were feeling sick.

'Memma were sent here with orders from her king to extinguish the volcano. In doing so, the whole island will be flooded. I saw it in a dream. We're to be sacrificed for the good of the many, or so she says,' I added.

The hunter took this in, looking from me to Memma.

'Don't you see?' I asked him. 'We've been tricked. The whole island will be lost. Every creature will be washed away and drowned, just like the sunken city down there.'

Rose Red stepped away and snatched Memma's logbook from her hands. 'What are you writing about us? That we're all stupid and ignorant? Just because we're not of your world?'

Dog-boy gently pulled the book from Rose Red's grasp. 'No, it int like that at all, Rose. After all she's done for us, how can you say such a thing?'

He passed the logbook back to Memma but kept his distance. I could see doubt playing over his face as he thought.

It all made sense to me now. 'That's why you went with Stoat. You were calculating your chances of completing your expedition successfully. You had a look at us and it dint look like we were up to much, growing vegetables and shovelling snow. But you had to come back to us when you found out Stoat were just using you. And then all that time in the library you were pretending to work alongside us when you knew all along what you had to do. How could you?'

'T'wasn't entirely one-sided,' Memma argued back. 'I taught thee how to conduct valorous science and how to fly above this frozen island you've been maroon'd on all these generations.'

Dog-boy, quick as ever, became sure of himself. 'Snow is right, you used us and tricked us,' he said furiously.

I put a hand to his shoulder but he threw it off. 'Leave me alone.'

He walked away, shoulders slumped. Rose Red ran behind him, and I looked after them helplessly. When I turned back, Memma had her sharp gaze turned on me. 'Thou hast no idea who thee are, do thee, child?'

'What are you talking about?' I said, angry still, but now nervous as well.

'I saw it when you showed me your fire-mountain coins. Thou art coins of the court, and only used by the royal family.'

'Those are stolen coins,' I shot back.

Memma shrugged. 'Whatever their origin, it maketh no diff'rence now thou art found.'

'What do you mean, *I'm found*?'

'T' maketh sense,' Memma continued casually. 'Thee hast the look of the royal family. Thy hair, and the shape of thy eyes. Thee don't look like anyone 'round hither, or haven't thee noticed? Your mother wast the runaway princess, the daughter of our King Augustus. She'd fallen in love with a gardener and ranneth hence from the palace in disgrace. When 'twere discovered the princess wast carrying a child, the king searched the four corners of this earth looking f'r it.'

I suddenly remembered the riders that came to the chateau on my last dark night in the tower. The horses snorting, trying to clear icicles from their nostrils in the bailey. The clink of metal shoes on paving. The footsteps in the hall outside my room, heavy ones like those of men in riding boots.

'The riders who came to the chateau that night . . .' I said, turning to the hunter.

'I remember,' he said, arms crossed over his chest.

'Sent by the king, nay doubt,' Memma said. 'He looked everywhere, even on this god-forsaken island at the bottom of the world.'

There were more than a hint of scorn in her voice but when I looked her in the face it had its usual smooth and slightly absent-minded look.

I was feeling dizzy and ill and the hunter caught my arm as I swayed. Could Memma be telling the truth? Was I the granddaughter of the king who had so imperiously ordered a volcano doused so he could enjoy a longer spring? Whose own ancestors had raided and stolen golden coins from a peaceful city? My mother a runaway princess? It made a mad sense. Why I'd always been nicknamed Little Queen. The rumours were based on a scanty truth, long hidden. Had my stepmother known all along?

'The riders must have told Rain who you really were,' the hunter said, reading my mind. 'That's why she ordered you killed out of nowhere.'

I felt shocked but for the first time in my life, the missing pieces of my life were fitting together. I dint want it to be true but I knew it was. I knew it the same way I knew what the trees were saying and what Little Bear were thinking. I just knew.

'What happened to my father, the gardener?'

'He lost his head for consorting with the princess,' Memma said, as if it were of no particular note. 'Thou mother hadst wayward blood and some in the court are of the mind the royal line is better off without it. She was not missed beyond

163

the extent of the king's anger. The young prince is heir now. Though now that thee are discov'r'd alive, that will be thrown into doubt.'

'I have a cousin?' I said, almost breathlessly. Memma had lost interest.

'If you ruin my work here the king wilt nay be pleas'd,' she said. 'But 'tis of little note. He will send people to finish the scheme, based on mine observations.'

The hunter and I looked at each other in alarm.

'And I will include thy presence here in mine report to the king,' Memma said, resuming her note-taking.

I felt an upwelling of fury. Not for myself, but for the way this king had had my father cold-heartedly executed and my mother hunted down. And if that weren't enough, now he'd be washing a whole island away because he felt like it. As had sometimes happened in my life, I felt a wave of power wash over me.

'You won't,' I told her. 'I forbid it.'

Memma did not immediately look up from her work but when she did, I caught a glimpse of hesitation in her clear gaze.

'I forbid you from including any mention of me in your reports, do you understand?'

Memma bowed her head. 'Yes, madam,' she replied, cowed.

'And I'll have my fire-mountain coins returned, if you please.'

Memma, keeping her eyes down, unzipped one of the pockets in her flying suit and handed over the pouch of my mother's remaining coins.

'I won't stop you from leaving, that would be cruel. But I'll not lend you any more assistance, do you understand?'

'Aye, madam,' Memma replied, again bowing her head.

Feeling like I'd squirmed out of my own body and left it standing there an empty shell, I walked away.

That evening the four of us sat quietly in our original lake-side camp. We were mourning Memma, though she weren't dead.

'Dead to me,' the hunter said, not one to abide disloyalty.

Dog-boy sat with his head in his hands, devastated at the loss of his friend and mentor. Rose's tear-stained cheeks were as red as her hair.

The hunter told them what Memma had told us.

'So you really are the Little Queen,' Rose Red breathed, an alarming look of awe on her face.

'I int nothing of the kind and if you treat me any differently knowing this, I'll regret I ever told you.'

'Yes, miss,' she replied.

I'd spoken sharply and hadn't meant to. Were I changed now? I remembered how I'd spoken to Memma. Was ordering people around as I liked in my blood? I struggled to set those worries aside for now because we needed to decide what to do.

Really, there was only one thing to do.

The volcano watched us put our balloons back together and prepare for flight, its column of hot gases and ash streaming upwards, disappearing into the low clouds. But now we knew, just like the people in the drowned city had known, that one day the volcano would settle and stop erupting and the clouding over would clear.

Memma objected to our leaving now, seeing we meant it.

'Do not defy thy king, I warn thee,' she told us, skating around on the ice.

'Int my king,' the hunter said crossly under his breath, and did not pause in his work.

I paid her no attention, batting her away, as did the hunter and Rose Red, so she pestered Dog-boy the most. He put his head down to the re-sewing of his balloon and turned his back on her but I were worried. Poke sat by and growled at Memma occasionally which made her keep a safe distance but it dint stop her lecturing Dog-boy.

'Hark to the science, boy. T' dost not forswear. All thy calculations wast correct, I didn't manipulate those in any way. Thee hast reached the right answer ev'ry time. Thee don't belong hither 'mong these ignorant people, thee shouldst attendeth university. Doth thee knoweth what that is? I shall recommend thee to the royal university, the king himself shall recognise thy talents when I tell him how thee helped me to returneth the sun to the sky. We will proceed with the grand scheme together.'

At this Poke lowered his muzzle and growled softly at the bird-woman. 'The science tells the truth,' she finished, desperate now.

Dog-boy stood and turned to confront her. We all looked up from our work, the hunter half-rising in case the boy were about to lose his temper and start throwing his fists at the tiny woman.

'I never doubted science tells the truth but it's people who have to decide what to do with that truth. Just because something can be done, doesn't mean it should be.' Memma opened her mouth to argue some more but Dog-boy went on. 'I know melting the lake would pour water into the volcano but we don't know what might happen after that, and neither do you. Miss Snow's right in that it will let loose an amount of water that could devastate the island. But only a god could know exactly, and I never met any of those. Not in a mountain or a tree or a balloon or anything else.'

'Dog-boy is right. Just because we can do it, doesn't mean we should,' Rose Red said loyally.

'More explorers from the Restoration shall cometh following me and the volcano will be dowsed,' Memma shot back defiantly, talking to all of us now. 'Wait until the king hears of how I hast been treated. He shall sendeth an army to reclaim the Restoration's honour.'

I raised my eyebrows. 'An army? What do you think of that, Little Bear?'

She hardly ever did it, but to oblige me she stood on her hind legs, rising to her full height of one and a half men, opening her mouth and roaring for good measure, a sound that echoed around the lake crater.

Memma slid away over the ice on her knees, taking cover in her basket with her instruments.

Flying home

We were soon ready to launch our balloons and go home. They had each been reassembled and preliminary checks had been done. Dog-boy was to be chief pilot now and he were taking his responsibility seriously. I was glad it seemed to have lifted his spirits, or at least distracted him. On launch day we left Memma watching us from next to her balloon, kneeling on the frozen lake, looking very small. I refused to feel sorry for her. She had enough catalyst left to carry her home and I hoped she would stay quiet about me but dint have much faith in her keeping her word once she were away.

As we ascended from the frozen lake surface we could see the story of fire-mountain portrayed in the sunken city. That part had not been damaged by the earthquakes and for a moment I believed in a fire-mountain god.

I looked over the edge of my basket to see if I could spot my bear. We'd bade them leave, Little Bear and the baby bear and Poke, me and Dog-boy explaining at length that they had to walk back the way they came, giving them their last pats along with a big bowl of porridge for the cub. Poke was reluctant but Little Bear gave him a nudge and the trio left the lake edge together to begin the long walk back the way they'd come.

I turned my attention to flying as we approached the clouding over. Lady landed with a crunch of her talons on the edge of my pine-needle basket, startling me. She turned around in the bow, to face the front, flicking her feathers smooth.

'Come to supervise the flying again?' I asked her. 'I'm grateful for your company, Lady, though you're not as friendly as my bear.'

To get home we had to fly south, against the air rivers that had brought us north so easily. If we flew higher, Dog-boy said, we would find one of the southerly air rivers. These were faster and colder and more dangerous, but if we flew at night we could use the stars to navigate and be more sure of our bearings without Memma's instruments to guide us. It were a risk Dog-boy had calculated carefully and we placed our faith in him. What he lacked in experience he made up for in the knowledge he'd soaked up like a sponge from Memma. He were taking her betrayal the hardest, for he'd felt closest to her, and had placed the most trust in her. But he'd turned his mind to the puzzle of getting us home and I saw in him the potential to be a great leader. I was ready to follow him, though the way ahead was difficult and dangerous.

We were all looking ahead. We weren't to know what was about to happen.

Our reduced fleet climbed steadily, the landscape of snow-capped peaks and smoking volcanos spread out beneath us like one of Cook's best tablecloths. Dog-boy's bell tolled as he entered the cloud cover and I trimmed my wings as I followed last. A few minutes later I heard Dog-boy enter the sky above. I were almost level with Rose Red and the hunter as my balloon passed through the last of the wispy tendrils of stratus and we sailed free above the clouding over.

This time, instead of holding our altitude, Dog-boy put out flags to continue our ascent. We dropped some more weight from our sandbags and drifted up into the thin blue air high above the clouds. It became steadily colder and we layered on all the many furs and goat fibre coats that Rose Red had made us. Dog-boy had given strict orders to cover every part of our skin, since frostbite would take hold immediately at the heights we were going to. We were also to keep eating the rations we'd packed. The more we ate, the warmer we'd be and the lighter our balloons would become.

We rose through the layers of air rivers, Dog-boy checking his charts and putting out his flags to keep us all close together. Briefly, we were close enough to have a shouted conversation. The air had stilled as we'd passed out of one river and were yet to enter the one above.

'We need to go higher,' Dog-boy shouted.

'We're already at our upper limits,' Rose Red called back. Her balloon had the best-functioning altimeter and she were in charge of logging our ascent.

'A little higher will bring us to the southerly-flowing air river, I'm sure of it,' Dog-boy shouted back.

The glowing disc of the sun was beginning to sink into the cloud cover at our backs, and the first star was already showing. Not a star but a planet, if I remembered rightly.

'We'll ascend,' I shouted. 'As Dog-boy says.'

'Yes, miss,' he shouted back. 'We'll be home before you know it!'

We all stoked our burners, gently drifting apart once again, and flew higher.

Finally I started to feel the wind rustling against the silks of my balloons, pushing my craft forward.

Dog-boy rang his bell and put out the flags for our course setting, and we were off.

If flying up until then had been like rowing a boat across a pond, now it was like a hawk diving-bombing a mouse in an open field. The wind whistled past, our silks flexing and cracking in the bigger gusts. Our baskets rocked to and fro and we strapped ourselves in as we'd been taught, lying low in the bottom. Even Lady hopped off her perch and made a nest in my furs, her feathers fluffed up against the biting chill.

My teeth began to chatter and I forced myself to wriggle my toes and fingers to warm them. The stars rose, just as they had on the chart in the great hall, and they were a wonder to see once again, like old friends come unexpectedly for dinner.

Rose Red signalled we were at the very highest point we could go safely, and we couldn't stay there long. We were flying now in what Memma told us was the dying zone, where there was barely enough oxygen to breathe. Here, the body started to burn energy for the smallest of movements and slowly a person's thoughts froze up. If we stayed too long the balloon silk would freeze and crack and we wouldn't be able to open our vents to descend. I had frozen to death before and I weren't planning on doing it again, so I tried to stay alert.

Our burners stayed lit and warm through the cold night. A full moon climbed through the cloud cover and lit the scene with grey light. It were so bright we could see each other and didn't need to toll our bells. Still we did because it was good company to hear the sound when the lonely wind were the only other sound to hear. There was a thrill in flying fast, like riding a sled down a steep snowy hill. We shifted our direction by trimming our wings and soon it became second nature to do so. I began to feel like a pilot in my bones, swept away with the joy of it. It was becoming nearly impossible to lift my arms, and my toes were numb and very far away, but the wind was singing now, not howling like a devil. I turned my head with the utmost effort to see the moon floating above us. *The moon was a balloon as well! A great glowing balloon lit from within. Was there a basket underneath, flying a huge god?* I wondered, and tried to see. There were lines in the dust on the great globe. Perhaps they led to a basket, hanging underneath.

Lady squawked, and walked along my arm, digging into my flesh with her talons. I noticed a small voice coming from the very base of my skull. It were quiet but stern. *Snow*, it said, *Your thoughts are getting frozen and strange. The moon is not a balloon. You're too high. You gotta get down.*

The voice was insistent, no matter how much I tried to ignore it. I looked to the fleet, but there was no movement in the other baskets that I could see. Rose Red was drifting dangerously off course, sailing away from us, and rising even higher. I reached for my bell, using all my strength. It were the hardest reach I ever made, and it were barely an arm's length. I tolled my bell as loud as I could, continuously. I kept ringing until I heard the others rouse and ring theirs as well. I put out flags for an urgent descent, and dampened my burner, at the same time pulling on the line that opened the vent to let warm air out of my balloon. I started to sink immediately but I were leaving the others behind.

I had an anxious wait, looking above, my gaze flicking to each of the balloons in turn. The moonlight was so bright I could make out the silk colours. Green and red and gold, shining dully.

Finally, each pilot began to descend. It was painstaking to watch. Rose Red, having drifted the furthest, took the longest to respond, her balloon moving sluggishly and then with a series of jolts. At least she was alive and pulling on lines, I thought. From one second to the next, I had slipped out of the fast-flowing air river, back into calm skies. I rang my bell and soon after heard three responses.

We slowly sailed together, until we were close enough to shout. Everyone was okay, though frozen to the bone. It weren't time to exchange stories, just to plan our next move.

'Did we fly far enough, Dog-boy?' I called.

'Short some way still, miss,' he called back.

Reports were that we had fuel enough for now, but we were stuck between air rivers. The one we wanted to catch was too high and the one below would take us in the wrong direction. 'Can we stay here?' I called to Dog-boy.

'No, miss,' he called back. 'We'll burn through our fuel and sit still in the same spot.'

Lady, who'd jumped back onto her perch, suddenly launched, her strong legs rocking my basket as she pushed off. Where was she going? She was flying toward a blank spot in the night sky. The north stars had disappeared. Was I having peculiar thoughts again? Seeing things that weren't there? I had time to wonder before my stomach dropped in horror. While we'd been talking and not paying attention, a giant section of the sky had been blocked by a storm. It were rolling onto us now that we'd hopped out of the rapid air-river. If we'd stayed up high, we'd have stayed ahead of it. And also died of cold. Now we were stuck between a frying pan and a fire.

The others had seen it. 'Descend!' Dog-boy shouted. 'As fast as possible. Shed all weight, open vent lines to maximum. We might still make it.'

It was a frenzy then of throwing all that we could overboard, leaving only those items we needed to stay alive, and even then there were difficult choices to make. Overboard went the biscuits and extra clothes and my knife. I watched them disappear through the cloud cover like pebbles in a muddy pond. The others did the same. We started descending so fast that my belly rose into my ribcage and my head became light. Lady landed with me again and together we clung to the edges of my basket.

We were too late though. The storm engulfed the balloon fleet, catching us like an avalanche on a steep mountainside. I lost sight of the others, though I heard their bells tolling, most likely of their own accord in the fierce wind. I strapped myself into my basket and held on for a wild ride.

A dangerous rescue

Memories came back to me as I sat in the belly of my basket, alone but for the hawklet. Of hiding under the table in Cook's kitchen, feeling the cold draft from the door opening and a family walking in, but all I could see were legs. One was a boy wearing too-big boots who would grow into the hunter. I remembered making friends with mice during the long years I were kept a prisoner by my stepmother, sharing my crumbs and teaching them tricks in the narrow shaft of light that crept across the floor of my tower cell. Of freezing to death after crossing a cold river. Of being shot through the chest with an arrow and dying right there on the crossroad at the edge of the city.

The cold was creeping in with long bony fingers, confusing my thinking and trying to get a grip on me. *How many times can a person die of cold?* I wondered.

The lines of my balloon creaked and the silks were stiff with ice. It were calmer, I noticed. The storm had passed. It had been fierce and short. Though maybe I'd just been spat out on the other side of it like a bad taste.

I opened my eyes, my lashes heavy with icicles. I'd never

been so cold on land as I felt then in the sky. Even frozen earth held warmth that a clear sky did not.

Where were my friends? Where was the hunter, Dog-boy, Rose Red? Had they been swept up into the heavens and lost? I peered over the frayed edge of my basket but the air was pale blue and as empty as a hollow heart. My chest hurt and it was hard to breathe which meant I was very high, probably grazing the very top of the dying zone. I could feel a bruise rising on my forehead. I must have passed out, either from the cold, or from a knock to my head.

Lady regarded me from her perch in the bow. She spread her wings, poised to take flight. To leave me.

'I need to move. I know,' I told her croakily.

It was one thing to set my mind to it, it was another to make my limbs do as I asked. Frozen to the bone, moving was agony. My skin was tight and burnt by wind and sleet, my tongue swollen to twice its size for want of water. I pushed myself to sitting in the stern of the basket and grasped the wing trimmer. If it wasn't broken there was hope yet.

One thing at a time. I tried to remember what I'd been taught.

When I pushed the lever, I felt the basket turn in response.

All well and good, Lady seemed to say, as she adjusted her balance. *But where are you going?*

The sky behind us was black with rolling clouds. The sky ahead clear.

'Away from the storm, Lady. That's the way open, that's the way we'll go. For now.'

I stoked my burner to warm the air in my balloon and fill out the silks. I tugged on the vent line and were relieved to feel that it wasn't frozen solid. I could still descend under control, rather than falling like a dropped china bowl. I tolled my bell loudly and often, stopping only occasionally to listen for a response. I checked my bearings. It were daylight and the sun was low in the sky. The trouble was, I couldn't tell if it were morning or evening low. I had to keep a watch on it to track it in the sky. I'd gotten turned around and around in the storm, like a riverboat riding rapids. In the middle of the horrible night, it hadn't been like flying but more like being an arrow shot from a bow. I shuddered. All I could do was hold on.

I rang my bell again. What hope was there of finding the fleet now? We'd probably been blown to the four corners of the compass. And if I weren't even sure of my bearings, how could I fly to where my friends might be?

And then I heard it. The faint toll of a balloon bell. Lady caught it too and launched into the air. Lacking a better idea, I followed, trimming my wings to sail after her. The way ahead was misty and murky. Tendrils of clouds had separated from the clouding over, drifting up and around me. But soon, looming more quickly than I'd expected, was another balloon. My heart filled with hope when I saw the green silks of the hunter's balloon. He was weakly tolling his bell from where he lay. I came as close as I dared, the silks of our balloons bumping together gently above us.

I called him urgently. His basket rocked in response before finally his head rose above the edge. Lady alighted there, brushing his face with her feathers in her landing.

'Not dead yet, Snow?' he croaked.

'Who are you talken about, you or me?' I said. 'Because you look more dead than alive.'

I was crying, with relief, and cursed the empty air between us that prevented me reaching out to touch him. The tears froze on my cheeks and stiffened the skin around my mouth.

'Where are the others?' he asked.

'I don't know, but we're going to find them and then we're going to get some solid ground back under our feet, because I'm suddenly not so fond of flying as I were.'

'Agreed,' said the hunter.

Between us we worked out it was a morning sun, so we were drifting south. We had daylight to sail on and search for Dog-boy and Rose Red.

'We'll keep going until we run out of fuel,' I said. 'Toll your bell often, you hear me?' I told the hunter, who was looking drowsy again. 'Don't die, because I won't stand it.'

'Yes, Little Queen.' He only used my nickname when he was teasing me. I smiled though it made my frozen cheeks ache.

Night was falling and it was very cold again. It had been a long and anxious day. Without Rose Red's altimeter readings, we dint know how high we were but I was beginning to think we were dangerously near the dying zone once again. The air was feeling thin and moving was becoming more and more of a chore. I was just about to signal to the hunter that we should descend when I heard a bell. It was faint and far away, hard to hear over the creaking of my basket and the snapping of my silks, but there it was again.

I looked to Lady. 'Can you show me where?' I asked her. 'Like you did before?'

I was wondering aloud but the hawklet tipped her head on the side, just as Little Bear did sometimes, and then opened her wings and soared away. She weren't sure at first, circling just above my balloon, and I wondered if she'd understood what I was asking of her. Slowly she seemed to get her bearings and then she flew away ahead and to port. I put out my flags and tolled my bell and soon the hunter were following.

Lady led us higher. I couldn't drop any more weight, so I put more precious fuel on the burner. And then I saw them, the gold and red silks of Dog-boy and Rose's balloons, drifting so high it would be dangerous to reach them. I tolled my bell madly and received only the weakest of replies. Soft and quiet and a long way off. It was too far for them to see but I put out flags telling them to urgently descend.

I waited but there were no responding flags. They'd been too high for too long. Death was creeping up on them. But so were we.

Feeding more fuel into my burner I got it burning bright and soon I was gaining altitude and closing the gap. The hunter followed me.

It seemed an age before I drew close enough to shout and when I did I finally saw movement in Dog-boy's basket. He pushed himself upright and tried to tell me something. I sailed as close as I could, but it weren't close enough to hear him.

'You have to descend, Dog-boy!' I told him. 'Right away!'

Finally I managed to hear his croaking reply. 'I can't leave Rose.'

What did he mean? I scanned the sky above. All of the lines on Rose's balloon were caked with ice and frost. Even her basket was white with it. There was no movement inside.

'She's too light,' Dog-boy called. 'Her vent is frozen shut and she's ascending.'

'We need to get more weight to her, Dog-boy. Can you throw something across?'

'I tried,' he said. 'I threw all my fuel blocks and missed every one.'

'Has she spoken to you?'

'Not for some time now,' he replied, so quietly I could barely hear him. 'But I'm not leaving her.'

I was thinking as hard as I could. We dint have much time before everyone's thoughts were frozen, along with our fingers and toes.

'Dog-boy, we need to get a line across to her. Maybe we can tow her down with us as we descend.'

I saw Dog-boy's hand grip the edge of his basket.

'Miss, I can't throw. I've missed every time. My hands are frozen.'

There had to be another way.

'Find a line, Dog-boy, and make it a light one,' I shouted. I was becoming hoarse and my lungs hurt from sucking in the freezing air to yell across the distance. 'Hold it as high as you can.'

I turned to the hawklet. 'Can you do it, Lady?' I asked her.

In answer, she dropped off the side of my basket and flew to Dog-boy, snatching the line from him and flying to Rose's basket, landing inside. It was too far to see what she did but there was no movement in the basket.

Rose is dead, I thought. There's no hope. If she couldn't secure her end of the tether, there would be no way to pull her down with us.

Dog-boy was leaning over the edge of his basket now, holding something out to Lady. It looked like a mouse, but where had he found a mouse in the middle of the sky?

My thoughts were getting strange again, I realised. *The air is too thin. I'm starting to see things.* But whatever I was seeing, Lady seemed to see as well, and still with the tether in her talon, she flew back to Dog-boy, having looped the rope around one of Rose's balloon stays.

I couldn't believe it. What a clever bird.

'Descend, Dog-boy,' I yelled, 'As fast as you can.'

As soon as I was sure he was going down, gently and awkwardly tugging Rose's balloon behind his, I followed. The hunter had stayed slightly below us and soon we levelled up with him.

I took over the piloting, putting out flags for our heading and continuing to slowly descend but it wasn't long before Dog-boy rang his bell three times. I looked around and saw he was stuck, his flag was out for not enough weight. The red and gold balloons were drifting higher again.

Racking my brain for a plan, I levelled off. There was movement in Dog-boy's balloon, rummaging around, his basket rocking from side to side. I couldn't tell what he was up to. Soon it became clear, all too clear, what he were planning.

The hunter realised first. 'No, Dog-boy,' he shouted through the thin air. 'It's too dangerous!'

Whether or not the boy heard, it dint stop him. Dog-boy had tied himself to the end of the tether and was climbing onto the edge of his basket. He'd attached himself to the tethering line with a kind of improvised harness like the one he'd made for Poke to tow Memma through the snow. He was going to use his own body weight to bring Rose Red back to earth. Soon, stepping off the edge of his basket, he was hanging in midair underneath Rose's balloon, causing her basket to rock and tip.

Lady launched from my balloon and flew in circles, calling out in alarm.

I had my hand over my mouth in horror. It was too terrifying to watch.

Dog-boy's golden balloon floated free of his weight, spinning gently so we could see Poke's sigil as it rose gently to the edge of the sky. Up and up it went, freed of the weight of Dog-boy. Soon it would be lost.

Now Dog-boy hung from the tether rope and with his weight added to Rose's they were descending, and faster than it was safe.

'Blasted heck!' the hunter shouted.

They passed us after a few moments, Dog-boy struggling to hold on, spinning in circles at the end of the line. I trimmed my wings and opened my vent to follow them down, my heart thudding with dread.

The descent

$\gg\!\!-\!\!-\!\!\rightarrow$

Dog-boy clung with frozen hands to the tether line, wondering whether it would be worse to look up or down. He decided on doing neither and instead concentrated on hauling himself up to Rose Red's basket. Once there he would climb inside and get her burner going again. Preferably before the balloon made the hardest of hard landings. He wrapped his legs around the rope beneath him and prayed his knots held. Hand over hand he inched his way up. His gloves were slippery, but without them he'd lose his fingers to frostbite. The rope was just like the one that had kept Memma's balloon tethered to the square. The same rope Rose had taught him to break and re-knot that he'd practised doing over and again all those nights ago in the city. He'd sat close to Rose with his elbow bumping hers and their knees touching as she showed him what to do. She'd been so close then he could see the creases in her lips and the fine hairs on her cheekbones. But it had been long before then that he fallen in love with Rose Red. Maybe it had been when he'd first seen her in the damp alley, struggling with her cart, her red hair spilling out of her hood. And then instead of being frightened or repulsed by his missing eye, she'd asked him rudely how he'd lost it, as if he'd carelessly misplaced it while washing his face, setting his eyeball aside like a pair of spectacles. He tried not to laugh at the memory for he needed his strength for climbing. He remembered Rose's arm around his shoulders when he'd found out about Memma's deceit. How light and warm and perfectly fitting it felt. How she put her forehead close to his own and told him, *Things will surely come right again.* And how he loved to watch her hands at work, a needle between her fingers and the frown she wore when she was concentrating. The problem was that the only way he knew how to show her he loved her was to argue with her. Sometimes, he had to admit, he deliberately drove her crazy because he was happiest when he was with her, and if that meant arguing, then that's the way he'd have to have it. He hauled himself up again, hand over hand, gripping the rope between his thighs.

Don't look down, he told himself. *And don't look up, neither.* He was terrified of what he'd find when he reached the basket. If Rose Red was dead, all the life gone from her body, because of him and his harebrained following of that bird-woman, he dint know what he would do.

Don't think about that neither, he told himself. *Sooner you get there, the sooner you can fix things.*

The last part was the trickiest. The basket rocked, unbalanced by his weight on the tether rope. He had to pull himself over the edge of Rose's basket without tipping everything, including her, into thin air. He got one hand to the top edge of the basket, and a toe to the bottom and with the last of his strength, just like climbing a sewer ladder, he swung himself into the basket, landing on top of a limp and lifeless Rose Red.

The top of the clouding over was fast rushing up at them. That meant it would be a close-run thing to get the balloon air heated enough to carry them to a soft landing.

First things first, Dog-boy told himself. *I gotta get this burner going to save us both.* While he did that with one hand, he shook Rose with the other.

'Rose Red, c'mon, wake up. Rose Red, do you hear me?'

There was no response. Working quickly in the cramped confines of the one-person basket, Dog-boy checked the lines and tolled the bell to signal he were okay, for now. The burner, which had been completely cold, started again, and he bent to blow on the small flame, pausing to glance over the edge of the basket to see how fast they were falling.

A soft voice came from behind him. 'Lucky we're both small.'

'Rose! You're alive,' Dog-boy said, pulling her into a tight hug.

'I'm glad to hear it. That were a lot of trouble to go to if I was dead,' she said with a weak smile. 'I'm very thirsty. Do you have any water?'

'None on me, Rose Red. I were a bit busy climbing a rope in mid-air to save your life to think of bringing you a glass of water as well.'

Rose smiled again. 'It's good to see you too, Dog-boy.'

She had the strength to joke but none else to spare. Dog-boy could see she was in a bad way. Her breathing was light and fast and her skin was clammy.

With the burner going well and the silks slowly thawing and filling out, Dog-boy needed to fly the balloon. To do that he needed to swap places with Rose.

'Can you move?' he asked her.

In reply, Rose lifted her hands but could not move her arms or legs, so damaged was she from the cold and exhausted from her ordeal.

So Dog-boy, small as he was, got his arms around her and with some shuffling that caused the bath-shaped basket to rock alarmingly, he managed to settle Rose in the bow, her knees drawn up, and get into the stern of the craft so he could handle the controls. He didn't have time to set a course, and they were going down anyway. Where they landed would be luck.

'Hopefully not the side of a mountain,' Dog-boy said under his breath.

'I heard that,' Rose said. 'You're too good a pilot to crash now. You can do it, Dog-boy. I believe in you.'

'That's one of us then,' Dog-boy replied with uncharacteristic humility.

And then they entered the clouding over and there was nothing to do but fly blind.

As we finally passed through the infuriating blindness of the clouding over, I leaned over the edge of my basket desperately searching the sky below for Rose's red balloon.

And there it was, still descending fast, but Dog-boy seemed to have climbed up the tether and brought the balloon under control. At least he weren't hanging in mid-air anymore.

'There they are!' I called, though the hunter was not close enough to hear me. So instead I rang my bell and, for the first time in what seemed like a century, I got two replies. I could breathe again and with each inhalation relief thawed my heart. It felt like coming in from the cold and setting aside a heavy fur coat.

But our troubles weren't over yet. We followed Dog-boy's rapid descent, but we were a lot slower. I trimmed my wings to follow as best I could, the hunter following in my wake.

In my desperate search to find Rose's balloon I had hardly noticed where we were, but I looked now and it was not a promising sight. We were descending over a field of lumpy blue-white ice that extended as far as I could see, from horizon to horizon, and that were no exaggeration. I couldn't make sense of it. Even if it was the largest lake on the island we should have been able to see the edges of it from the air. What could it be?

And then it struck me. We were flying over the frozen sea, and mercy knows where and how far the storm had taken us. We were about to land in a desert of ice.

An icy desert

With skill far beyond his age and experience, Dog-boy landed Rose's balloon softly, sliding to a halt on the lumpy sea ice with red silks billowing around them. He allowed himself a moment to close his eyes and feel relief wash over him. His arms felt like lead and his thighs stung with rope burn and frostbite. But there was no movement from Rose Red. Dog-boy sprang into action once again. He took down the burner and reassembled it on the ice and dragged in the silks to make a tent over the basket. He needed to warm Rose up as fast as he could.

We landed shortly after Dog-boy but not as close as we'd have liked, the hunter a little nearer than my clumsy, panicked descent. Scrambling free of my belts and ties, I ran toward the red fabric of Rose's balloon. Finding my way inside by pushing through what felt like acres of silk, I came to a small cave around the basket where Dog-boy and the hunter were rubbing Rose Red's hands and feet. She were as pale and cold as I'd been in my coffin.

'She were talking to me afore we landed,' Dog-boy said, wiping away tears impatiently. 'Now she won't wake up.'

'She needs warming up, boy. Don't fret. I've seen this before, once or twice,' the hunter said calmly, but I could tell by his frown that he were worried.

Rose Red lay in a bed of her red silks, coverings pulled up to her chin. She looked younger than she really was and glassy, like a sleeping infant. Slowly we warmed her up and when some colour ran into her cheeks and she murmured something about birds and ribbons and turned her head to the side, we started to feel like she was going to come back to us.

The air in the tent grew warm and I started to feel sleepy with it. I couldn't remember the last time I'd slept long and warm and deep. But before there could be sleeping, we needed to try and work out where in sweet heck we were.

Leaving the hunter with Rose Red, Dog-boy and I fought our way out through the swathes of silk to get our bearings. Dark were falling as we surveyed our landing site.

'The frozen sea,' Dog-boy said in awe.

'Sitting like crumbs on a plate.' I couldn't keep the fear from my voice. The wide-open space was making me dizzy. I needed a mountain or a river to find my way. Above the clouding over there were the sun and the stars. Here there was nothing at all to show us where we were. White above and white beneath. We were more lost now than we'd ever been.

We dragged the other balloons in close and pegged them down against the wind rising in the dark night and went back inside.

The hunter had revived Rose Red enough that she was sitting propped up against her basket and eating some biscuit soaked in water. She smiled to see us and reached out a hand for Dog-boy who took it in both of his and sat close beside her.

Rose Red's fingers and toes were black and blue with frostbite. I fretted for her fingers that were so skilled with needles and machines but she was not concerned.

'The hunter said they'll get better. And I'm lucky to be alive,' she added.

The hunter looked at me, asking what we saw out there.

I shook my head. 'Nothing in sight to give us our bearings. We could be in the middle of the great south land for all we know.'

'Where did the animals go when the sea froze over?' Rose Red asked. 'The penguins and seals and whales? Those that breathe air to live.'

'The sea int frozen over where Memma comes from,' Dog-boy said. 'They probably all went there.'

'It's not?' I said in surprise. 'What else did she say?'

Dog-boy shifted, but it weren't the cold ice he sat on making him uncomfortable. I hadn't been curious at all about where Memma came from before and I wondered why. Was I as ignorant as she'd accused me of being?

'It was named the Restoration lands by the king who claims credit for building the civilisation that rose up after the clouding over. And now it's all land he controls, as far as I could understand her anyway.'

'And I suppose he keeps all this land under his control with an army,' the hunter said.

'A big one,' Dog-boy said.

'No king is flying an army across the sea in balloons, or marching them across this ice, so I think we're safe for now,' the hunter said.

I thought of the ocean of deep and solid ice. In places it

was lumpy with waves but it seemed to me it was perfect for marching over. They could even make a road, if they had a mind to, and pull carts loaded with supplies along it. It were a solution even easier than loading an army into boats and sailing them across uncertain waters. I dint say anything in reply to the hunter, keeping my thoughts to myself for now.

I was aware through the night, in our close quarters, of Dog-boy stirring restlessly. I knew he was checking that Rose was still alive because I could see him in the cold dimness occasionally resting his head on her chest to listen for her light breathing. But there was something else on his mind as well and when he crawled out through the silks at first light, I threw off my blanket, leaving the hunter sleeping, and followed him.

It was still and cold, quite beautiful in a terrifying way, I were prepared to admit. The ice glowed, like it was lit by lamps from within, in all of the white-blue spectrum of colours, everything imaginable from turquoise to lavender. Now and then there were loud cracks that I took to be the vast ocean underneath the pack ice shifting as if in protest at being smothered. There was no way to tell how thick it was. And unlike the frozen lake, which had been perfectly clear, the ice under our feet was frothy, like frozen milk. It were making us all nervous.

Dog-boy was walking in circles, climbing atop one wave after another, jumping off and running to the next one. He spent some time in stillness, appearing to be deep in thought.

I was worried. We had biscuits to last a few days but it would be light rations and that was no good for Rose's recovery. She needed goat milk and red meat, according to the hunter. But it couldn't be helped. We had meagre equipment having had to lighten our balloons to reach the high air river. I mourned the loss of my knife, but there weren't any rabbits out here for using it on, I told myself.

Worst of all we were carrying hardly any water. Our flight plans always had us descending onto land where there was snow to melt. We were standing on an ocean of water, but it was too salty to drink. So we were going to go thirsty and no way around it.

I watched Dog-boy while we nibbled our breakfast biscuits. Finally he was ready to share his thinking with us.

'We follow the waves,' he told us. 'I'm thinking they were being blown by the wind when they froze and we know most of the wind comes from the south, bringing all those storms with it, so if we follow the waves, they'll guide us home.'

'I'm not sayen it's not a bright notion, boy,' the hunter said carefully. 'But we don't know where we landed. Maybe we came down north of the island and then where will we be but flying off the edge of the ice, ifen it has an edge?'

'I thought of that, and it is a risk. But I've been tryen to remember how that storm tossed us around and if anything, it drove us into the south. Otherwise, how could it be so cold?'

The hunter humphed in agreement.

'So the real danger,' Dog-boy added, 'is that we're in the middle of the frozen south and our home is too far to fly to.'

Rose Red put her hand over her mouth in fear.

'But I think we're closer than that,' he added hastily. 'These waves look like ocean waves to me, this int pack ice which is all boulders and slabs.'

'How do you know?' I asked.

'From looking, that's all,' he admitted. 'From sitting on the city walls and watching the sea when I were small, before it froze over. And from books and pictures.'

I'd noticed Dog-boy seemed taller since we'd left the chateau, and there was something different about the way he was carrying himself, in spite of Memma's betrayal. I for one were willing to place my trust in this one-eyed boy.

'We follow the waves,' the hunter agreed.

Rose Red nodded as well, her eyes on Dog-boy.

We had fuel enough for one more flight, though none of us knew how long it would last. To lift two people in Rose's balloon would take more fuel so we divided our last fuel bricks accordingly and started the process of launching.

Having come down in such a muddle, my lines took quite an effort to untangle and while my hands worked my mind wandered. Would Memma obey my order not to reveal where I was, or would she defer to the higher authority of my grandfather the king? I suspected she'd favour the king, given the way she'd looked at me and the mention of my wayward blood. Though she was an explorer, she was a loyal subject, and her aeronautic training taught her to obey the orders she were issued, I supposed. If she'd launched her balloon as soon as we'd left the lake, she could be back in her land by now, though I had no idea how long the flight would be.

'Dog-boy,' I called. 'How long would it take Memma to fly back to the Restoration lands? Did she ever tell you?'

Dog-boy replied grimly. 'I been thinking the same, miss, and I reckon it could be only a matter of days in her fast craft.'

I bade my fingers to work faster, following the lines and getting them all laid out straight. 'We've got to hurry then,' I told my companions. 'We might be racing an army.'

The weather stayed calm and mercifully still and soon we were launched and back in formation. This time Dog-boy led in Rose's balloon with the hunter and I following. The plan was to remain under the cloud so we could follow the waves. If we hadn't reached land by the day's end we would ascend through the cloud cover to get a bearing from the stars. It weren't likely we'd have the fuel to do that, so we were pinning our hopes on spotting land before we lost the light again.

If I weren't suddenly so worried about invading armies and whether we were south of the south pole somewhere, it would have been a beautiful day of flying. The wind pushed us along gently and we were able to fly slightly across it to follow the waves.

I was immensely relieved when Dog-boy's bell rang out and the flag went up for land ahoy. Peering through the haze I saw the rough and rugged coast of our own island dead ahead. Relief rushed through me. It was unmistakeably home. As we came closer, the mountains rose into view and soon we were flying over familiar territory once again.

But we weren't going home to the chateau, not yet. It was painful but we dipped our wings and glided down toward Fox's stinking city.

Mayor Fox and the stinking city

>>——>

Mayor Fox was the man I'd almost made the mistake of marrying. I'd loved him a little back then, but if Fox did something for someone, there was always something in it for himself. By marrying me, he would have had a share in the chateau. As well as the ownership of me, for that was how he viewed things. And when I finally saw that for myself, I left him at my own engagement party.

Back then we were almost of a height, him with dark hair always neatly cut and a clipped moustache above his top lip. Now I stood taller than he, and his hair was streaked through with silver.

We were ushered into his plush office. When he saw me he took a step back and bowed. This were part of how he mocked me and it dint mean anything, I reminded myself. His manner had the effect of making you think he was doing you a favour, when in fact he'd somehow made you do exactly what he wanted. I put my guard up.

'Little Queen,' he smiled. 'Still as beautiful as the day you left me. And the hunter, I see,' he said, holding out his hand. 'Never far away.'

The hunter shook Fox's hand though he'd clearly have rather not.

We still wore our flying suits and furs which were worse for wear after all our travels. We'd only stopped at an inn long enough to quench our thirst and eat a warm meal, after landing in a field just outside the city. Unnoticed, luckily, except for some crows who were startled into cawing flight by our arrival out of the sky. We left Rose Red by a roaring fire at the inn and Dog-boy there to look after her.

Fox wiped his hand on a handkerchief after touching ours, not bothering to hide his distaste.

'Sit, sit,' he said, indicating two velvet chairs opposite his desk that were sure to be spoiled by our sitting on them. I sat.

'What can I do for you?' he continued.

'It's a long story, do you have the time?' I said, straightforward.

'For you, anything,' he said, smiling tightly through the words he dint mean.

I told him, as quick as I could with as few diversions as I could manage, about Memma and the grand scheme and that an army was on its way to invade our island.

Fox's moustache twitched as he listened. He sat back in his chair and crossed and uncrossed his legs. When I finished he put his fingertips together in a steeple.

'Let me see if I've heard you correctly, Snow, for at times you hurried and skipped over some details that may be more pertinent than you believe.'

I dint know what pertinent meant but I weren't going to give him the satisfaction of sayen so.

'You have discovered that your grandfather is a king in

196

command of what sounds like a huge empire and you, your true mother having died, are the rightful heir to his throne?'

'That int the bit of the story that matters, Fox, and you know it,' I shot back. 'The part that matters is that some person who calls himself a king is sending an army to invade and occupy this island, just as he's done to countless others. And we have to stop him.'

'And how do you propose we do that, Little Queen? Or should I call you princess now? Princess Snow sounds quite striking, doesn't it? Explains why you feel you can order people to do your bidding just like that.'

His words stung me, as he'd known they would. He went on. 'And to think I might have been your prince if we'd married. Maybe I shouldn't have let you run away from me, Little Queen.'

'You dint have a say in my staying or going, Fox, and you know it. We need to raise an army and meet them on the ice,' I went on. 'And you have men, I know you do.'

'I have a few city guards who can barely fight their way out of sleep let alone face an invading force. No, princess, I think we should view the arrival of King – what did you say his name is? Augustus? – as an opportunity. Why fight a battle when you can win over your enemy with goods and services?'

I was shocked.

'Are you serious?' the hunter said, rising from his chair.

I held my hand out, indicating the hunter should stay calm. 'I should have known you wouldn't have the heart to defend your people,' I told Fox. 'How do you know what kind of ruler he is? By all accounts he's ruthless and power-hungry.'

'How do *you* know?' Fox countered. 'If he's your flesh and

blood, I'd wager he's a worthy soul who likes to think he rules with a velvet glove.'

This felt like an insult but I weren't sure why. 'You're willing to risk finding out by lying down and playing dead?'

'Snow, as you well know, I am not a fighter. I prefer to befriend my enemies and make them my allies.'

'You're fooling yourself this time, Fox. What do we have to trade? Some cheese and a few specks of gold hard-dug out of a mountain? That won't be enough.'

'Ah, but you said it yourself, princess. We have a lot more than that. We have a volcano that they want. What did you say? And a lake to douse it with? Sounds fanciful to me. But if there's one thing we do know, it's how to survive in the cold. I'd warrant we can safely provide guiding services for an army up to a frozen lake. As well as furs and meat and donkeys.' Fox made a show of doing calculations in his head. 'It will cost him, of course.'

The hunter stood abruptly. 'We're done here, Snow.'

I rose in agreement.

'We will not be surrendering fire-mountain, or letting any army walk anywhere on this island,' the hunter said as we left the room.

'You and whose army, hunter?' Fox laughed.

We returned to our inn and told Dog-boy and Rose Red what Fox had said. Dog-boy weren't at all surprised, having lived in the city all his life.

'Always in it for coin, that one,' he said.

'We can't fight an army by ourselves,' Rose Red said, her eyes wide with horror.

'Of course we can't,' I told her.

'But we do control the mountain pass that leads to fire-mountain. So we can make it difficult for them to cross,' the hunter said. 'That won't take an army.'

'They can fly over in balloons,' I pointed out. 'Memma knows where it is, they'll just land on it and for all we know, blast the dam open and douse the volcano that way.'

'Then what do you suggest?' Dog-boy asked.

'We have to meet them on the ice,' I said.

Snow visits the trees

Quickly replenishing our fuel supplies from the city, we hurried back to our balloons and flew to the chateau. I had a moment to notice how flying was just something we did now, almost without thinking. Although the balloon crafts were dangerous, and we'd come close to tragedy, flying a balloon up the mountain was a lot quicker than walking, and I was grateful for that.

We were home the same day, descending and landing in the bailey one by one.

After a bath and clean clothes, I walked around running my hands over the walls and patting the animals until I felt like my feet were properly back on the ground. I was disappointed in Fox, of course, but it were no real loss because what he said about the city guards was true. They were not an army.

The more I thought about it, the more certain I became that I was right about not waiting for the king's army to make it to the high passes and meeting them there. If we did that, the fight was already lost. Once they were here, it would be too late. They had to be turned back on the ice. Once and for all.

But I had no idea how to do that. Our people were skilled

in milking goats and growing food and building walls. And even though the chateau was full to overflowing, I knew that an army, though I'd never seen one, was made up of hundreds or thousands of fighting men marching and carrying and dragging their killing machines along with them. The vision made my blood run cold.

We'd hardly been back at the chateau for a moment when the watch rang the bell wildly. Running out into the bailey, the gate swung open to Little Bear and her cub and Poke, come to find us after walking the length of the island once again. Dog-boy ran to his friend and they rolled around in the snowy drifts in the bailey until Poke was worn out, which dint take long after their huge journey. I went to Little Bear and scratched her ears as she liked while her cub climbed up my legs until I gave him his pats as well. Watching it all from the chateau walls were Lady and her brothers, and circling above I noticed the hunter's falcon, come for a rare visit.

It were always when I had my hand in Little Bear's scruff, the thick fur around her neck, that matters became clear to me. Without trying, without thinking, I knew what I had to do.

But first the bears and the dog needed feeding and for that we went to see Cook.

The kitchen was warm as always, the big stove burning bright and occasionally misbehaving and blowing clouds of smoke like the dragon I always imagined it to be. Cook was rubbing balm into Rose Red's fingers and toes, making her wince. Dog-boy sat close by, as he always was these days. And they were arguing less, now they were clearer in their understanding of each other.

Cook directed one of her helpers to feed the animals. When their bellies were full they lay down in front of the fire, Little Bear taking up most of the spare space so Cook's people had to squeeze past her.

The hunter was looking at me closely as he cleaned his rifle at the table.

'I were thinking,' he said, 'you know there are a lot of people hiding out in the mountains who we could call on to fight for you. They'd come in if they knew their way of life were being threatened.'

'You're right, we may need them,' I agreed, half-heartedly.

'What, Snow? What are you thinking?' he asked me.

'I need to talk to the trees,' I told them all, aware it sounded like a mad thing to say.

My friends dint say anything in reply, waiting.

'This int just up to us,' I told them. 'If this king, my grandfather' – I were still almost choking on my words describing him that way – 'wants to add us to his so-called empire, the trees need to be told.'

'I'll come with you. When should we leave?' the hunter said, putting the parts of his rifle back together.

'Just me this time,' I told him. 'Something I have to do alone.'

Having half-risen from his chair, the hunter sat again reluctantly. 'As you wish, Little Queen,' he said, without any teasing in his tone.

I rose in the early hours of the following morning, just as I had when I first left the chateau with the hunter. He sat on the edge of our bed in the cold early light as I tied on my furs. 'Be careful, Snow,' he told me and kissed the palm of my hand.

Little Bear and her cub rose from the warm hearth of the kitchen stove and followed me out through the gates, the cub tripping over his sleepy feet. I dint bring a lamp for I wanted to feel the dark, and though my legs were longer now, the snow were deeper too. I wore my she-bear fur around my shoulders, and the dog-fur the hunter gave me long ago around my waist. Once again I missed the feel of my mother's knife in my belt and shook my head at stupidly throwing it over the side of my balloon in the storm. I must have been cracking up from the lack of air, like Memma had been when she'd thrown her strongbox overboard. Remembering Memma pulled up a host of bad feelings, but I told myself there weren't anything I would have done differently. We rescued her, we freed her from Stoat, and then we became mired in a plot that were way bigger than we'd imagined. She took advantage of our trust, and that was what hurt the most.

I felt my way along with my feet and my ears, my eyes being of little use. Little Bear went ahead and broke a trail for me. She knew where we were going. To the forest, to walk under the green canopy of leaves and ferns hung heavy with snow, to pass by gnarled trunks with their mossy fur coats and mushrooms strung like jewels. To hear the crunch of snow under my boots as the loudest sound, and let that quiet sink into my skull. The truth was that I hadn't heard the trees talking since I'd been running from my stepmother and hiding from the miners. I weren't sure they would speak to me now. Maybe it was a skill I'd lost over the years. Grown out of, like a pair of boots. If I couldn't tell the forest what was coming then they would be as unprepared as we'd been for Memma's deception. I had a duty to fulfil, if I still could. I was uncertain though, I couldn't hide that from myself. And it was part of why I'd come alone, refusing the hunter's company.

Lady joined our small party at first light, making her presence known with a low swoop over Little Bear's head, which annoyed the bear and made me smile secretly, before flying high to watch our slow progress. Even though we went in under the forest quietly we still disturbed a ruru perched in the lower branches just settling down to sleep for the day. The small owl took off indignantly on wings as quiet as a butterfly's.

There were risks in travelling alone and it weren't long before I felt the back of my neck prickle. I was being watched, and not by owls. Turning, I called into the silence of the forest. 'Come out, Stoat. I don't have time for being chased. I'll tell you what I'm about, there's no secret.'

Sure enough, after a moment a dark shape stepped out of the shadows.

'What's happened to the flying woman then? I take it her escape was your doing, Little Queen, one way or another?'

'She weren't yours to hold, Stoat, as you well know. You got what you wanted from her, and more'n that besides.'

Stoat shrugged in reply.

'Anyway, it's a long story, but she was here under orders, and now she's run to her king and he's bringing back an army. He's going to take what isn't his and I aim to stop him.'

'A king?'

'My grandfather, I'm not proud to say.'

Stoat, the scoundrel, the killer of girls, rocked back on his heels in surprise.

'I'm looking for an army to stand against him,' I went on,

'so I don't have time for you to put another arrow through my chest right now.'

Stoat took a few steps toward me and my hand went to my belt, missing my knife again.

'I'll have your back, if you need me,' he said unexpectedly. 'I've got no love for Little Queens but even less for kings. I live as I like and if that means sending this king on his way I'll fight on your side. Send a bird and I'll come,' he finished, flicking his gaze to the sky where Lady circled.

I nodded and turned, not worried about putting my back to him now we had an agreement. He'd keep his word on this, I felt sure.

To speak to the oldest trees I had a long walk ahead of me. Instead of climbing higher and higher, I'd stick to the valleys and steep gullies and find my way into the deepest and oldest parts of the forest that way. I listened as I walked, pausing often, but there was nothing to hear just yet.

I'd first noticed the whispering of trees when I were just a girl. I'd had the feeling as I passed under the branches that my arrival was expected and they were already discussing my business. I'd tried to ignore them then. Later, though they were still nosy, they became my friends, tellen me when the miners were headed back to camp and when I should get going soas not to be discovered missing. Those were pine needle forests, young and gushing and gossiping, but now I was looking for older trees, and I dint know how to listen to them.

I felt a weight settle in the pit of my stomach, like I'd swallowed a stone. What if I'd lost the knack? Maybe trees only talk to children. Or maybe only children have the ears to hear.

I fretted and walked, heading in no particular direction except darker into shadow. The dimmer the forest floor became, the taller the trees. The understorey was almost free of snow, all of it caught in the upper branches, just a few flakes drifting down through the maze of branches and leaves. I stopped often to admire mossy rocks, letting my eyes drink in the lush greens and soft textures. Here and there were stumps of trees so big that I could have laid down on them comfortably. The forest was always looking for an opportunity, so smaller trees and vines were growing up in place of the fallen giants, winding up toward the white light of the clouding over.

I made a camp in a valley with a gently flowing spring, not frozen just there in the warmth of the protected forest floor. I sat quietly outside my shelter for a long time before lying down to sleep, my whole body tuned in to listen. But still nothing. The cub shambled, rolling in dry leaves and clawing the trunks of trees, sharpening his claws. I hissed at him to be quiet and Little Bear turned her ears back on me. I felt bad and fretted through the night.

The next day we entered a forest of the largest trees I'd ever seen, reaching so high I could hardly make out the tops. Here the forest floor was covered in snow, the trees spaced out like dancers at a ball, politely giving each other elbow room. The cub was trying to climb each trunk, Little Bear growling at him each time to come down.

'Shush,' I told her crankily. 'I'm tryen to listen.'

Little Bear sat in the snow and raised her nose in the air, putting her ears back. Now she was really cross with me.

'Sorry,' I told her. 'Come on, we gotta get out under the sky. My head is bursting with listening to nothing.'

We headed uphill and soon cleared the edge of the forest. I climbed for the rest of the day, heading toward a rocky outcrop that looked out across the vast gully I'd been walking in. I climbed and worried, without feeling my legs carrying me. I felt disheartened, like I had when I came down from the volcano. I dint believe in gods, but I were sure I'd heard the trees whisper to me all that time ago. Could I have been imagining it? Was it my scared child-mind just making up stories and seeing things that weren't really there, like what happens when you fly too high? I thought I heard trees talking, when really I'd just been lonely and frightened.

Grasping for handholds, I pulled myself up the last few steps to a large flat rock. For a moment I paused on hands and knees, catching my breath. Little Bear joined me, shaking herself and turning to look for the cub who was close behind. And then I looked up. It was a view worth climbing for. All I could see was dark green forest, a vast valley sweeping down before me. As much green showing as snow caught in the branches, more green than I'd seen in years, even from my balloon. Lady landed on the rock beside me and, glancing down toward her, I couldn't believe my eyes. Maybe I'd climbed so high I were having those strange thoughts again.

Stuck blade-down into a crevice in the big rock was my knife. The same knife I'd tossed overboard during the storm. The one my mother had left me when she died.

I gently prised it from where it had stuck in the rock slab.

There was the strange inscription I'd long ago stopped trying to decipher. I saw it now with new eyes. It was still odd but since I'd become used to the way Memma spoke I could read it.

The trees off'r wisdom f'r those who canst heareth't. Stirreth not, little one, stayeth quiet and listen.

A sudden strong gust of wind rippled through the valley causing the treetops to stir. Like a wave it began at the far end of the forest and flowed up to the base of the cliff I stood on.

And finally I heard. The air was filled with the forest's whispers. Their wisdom had been there all along but my head had been too full of worry to hear.

I knew now what I had to do. I tucked my knife into my belt where it belonged. 'Time to go home, Little Bear.'

The princess and the king

I returned to the chateau and told my friends the plan that had been whispered to me.

Dog-boy launched his balloon the following morning to take the first watch. Rose and her helpers had worked hard to make him a new craft, just the same as the one that he'd had to abandon but with added improvements: a telescope was mounted on the basket edge, along with an altimeter of his own. He fitted new wings as well, shaped more like a bird's, he said. To slip through the air like one. The hunter would take the second watch, then Rose Red and then me. We would rotate until we saw the army approaching soas not to be caught unaware. I told Cook there would be a lot of mouths to feed, and she swung into action, assembling all her helpers and setting to work.

The long days had arrived which made fine flying weather with fewer storms than usual. When sleet and snow blew through, we kept the balloons grounded until the bad weather passed. We didn't need Memma's forecasting because we had the hunter. As he'd always insisted, he could feel when a storm were on its way without needing any instruments to tell him.

It weren't long before Dog-boy spotted the army approaching. From his hawk's-eye perspective he described it as a winding black snake, slithering across the ice below. The pace was slow due to the war machines which sat heavily on sleds that slid slowly over the ice. They were pulled by bedraggled horses, made skinny by the work, who hung their heads in their traces. Dog-boy's cheeks went red when he told us, landing in the bailey wildly ringing his bell.

'It's time,' I told everyone.

The balloons were launched and we flew to the coast. Rose Red and Dog-boy stayed aloft, hovering in place as best they could, while the hunter and I landed on the ice, between the approaching army and the beach they needed to cross to begin their march across country to the volcano.

I stood by my tethered balloon, keeping the burner hot to fill the silks with warm air so the army might see who they were facing. My sigil, a roaring Little Bear on dark blue silks, next to the hunter's soaring falcon on his green balloon. We stood together to face what was marching toward us.

Dog-boy and Rose Red, watching from above, told us what was happening with their flags. As the army's forward scouts arrived and saw us, they turned on their heels and quickly ran to the head of the main marching column. The report went back down the line then until it reached the king. Orders were issued and slowly the soldiers marched into lines in front of us. Row upon row of black-clad men holding shields and weapons of all descriptions. There were bows and rifles and staffs, even a few swords. Though the soldiers wore black, as they came closer we could see that their clothing was shabby. A few of the men were large but they served only to make the others look small. Some had skinny bare legs stuck into boots, and even from this distance we could see them shivering. They had not been properly equipped for a long, cold march into the south.

There was a wait while this unwieldy army organised itself in a defensive formation, readying themselves to wage a battle against me and the hunter and our balloons. It were a lot of trouble to go to and it took a long time. Officers walked up and down the line, shouting orders and occasionally issuing harsh reprimands.

My feet were getting cold and I stamped them on the ice to stir some blood.

'Hurry up,' the hunter said under his breath, not to me. He were impatient to get this over and done with. While we waited I glanced at his profile, his dark brows lowered for a fight, shoulders squared and feet placed firmly on the ice, arms crossed with rifle slung across his back. I tried to copy his stance, lifting my chin, not letting myself lean against my basket no matter how long the wait. I never expected there would be so much standing by in the face of battle.

Finally an opening formed between the rows of soldiers, the officers shouting orders and the soldiers shuffling aside, and the king's carriage appeared. It were unmistakably so, being golden and hung about with flags and embellishments, drawn by glossy black horses. A large man were helped down to the ice by two attendants each side. He was layered heavily with white furs and to my surprise he wore a crown. It sat heavily on his forehead and had the effect of pushing his eyebrows into a perpetual frown.

There was another pause while a banner was unfurled and held over the king's head. It were an impressive sight. Two lions stood on their hind legs over a golden crown, like the one the king wore, against an ornately decorated red, gold and white background.

'Very regal,' said the hunter dryly.

Now the moment had come, my stomach flipped. In watching the spectacle of the king's dismounting and approach, I'd forgotten that I were about to parley with my own grandfather.

'You got this, Little Queen,' the hunter told me. 'No joking now, I'm serious.'

Once again I lifted my chin, swinging my long braid over my shoulder and placing my hand on my knife. I walked forward to meet the king, the hunter staying two steps behind at my right shoulder.

Just before we were close enough to exchange words, a herald pulled out a horn and began to play a royal-sounding anthem. Glancing above, I saw Dog-boy had put out flags asking what was taking so long.

Finally the song was finished and yet another attendant stepped forward, shouting, 'All hail King Augustus the Third, Ruler of the Restoration Lands and all its Vassal States, and Commander of all the Highlands Armed Forces, Land, Sea and Sky.'

When he was finished the army shouted, *All hail!* obediently.

There was a pause then and I wondered if he'd finished. The king's party shifted uncertainly.

I supposed it was my turn. I stepped up, clearing my throat. 'All hail no one. I'm Snow and this is the hunter.'

The king's voice was gravelly and issued from his belly. 'So thou art mine own wayward daughter's child. I did search long and hard f'r thee on this damn'd island.'

'I dint know my mother, but what you say might be true, from what others have told me,' I replied.

'Ah, so we meeteth at last, granddaughter.'

'My family are here all around me, sir. I feel no allegiance to you or your land, or your rule,' I said bluntly.

The king reeled as if I'd thrown dung at him and thundered, 'Thy words, child, art treason! Wherev'r the royal feet tread becomes part of mine own empire. If't I hath chosen to tread hither, then all shall bow to me.'

'I think not, Grandfather,' I replied firmly. 'You have not set foot on the soil of this island and you never will.'

The king paused to make a show of chuckling, turning to all of his attendants until they pretend-laughed along with him.

Suddenly, the king stopped laughing and spoke through his teeth. 'Thee speaketh seditiously, child, f'r none stand with thou but f'r one bodyguard. Hast thee not noticed I hath an army at mine own back?'

'Oh, I have an army as well, sir. And I ask you now to turn your forces around and return to where you came from, and never think of crossing this body of water, be it ice or ocean, ever again.'

'Thee *asks* me?' the king replied, truly angry now, his face red and shoulders rising in anger. His attendants shrank away.

'I do, sir. Politely first, and then we shall see.'

In a gravelly grumble that made my blood run cold, the king spoke for the last time. 'Thee hath committ'd treason, princess, and at which hour this battle is wonneth, thee shall be'est carried in chains to the capital and executed.'

Having sentenced me to death before my trial, the king gave an order to one of his generals and began the process of climbing back into his carriage.

I turned to the hunter with raised eyebrows. 'I think our parley has finished.'

As we walked back to our balloons an order was bellowed out down the line.

'Nock! Draw!'

The hunter looked about in confusion. 'Who're they shooting at?'

The archer company had their bows drawn and were aiming high, as if there were an army lined up above them.

'I wouldn't, if I were you!' I called out.

'Loose!' shouted an officer.

A huge volley of arrows went out, turning the sky into a dark arch. The hunter and I took cover behind our baskets, but we needn't have bothered. As the arrows reached the peak of their flight, a huge flock of birds of every kind emerged from the sheltering belt of forest along the beach and plucked the arrows out of the air. It were one dark cloud meeting another, and the arrows disappeared, carried away in beaks and bills. One or two fell to the ice, harmlessly knocked out of the air.

This caused confusion among the soldiers, the archers looking to each other and their officers, some of them dropping to their knees in a crouch as if the birds were going to swoop.

'Not yet,' I said quietly.

We waited.

Next to step forward were the foot soldiers, brandishing their assorted weapons with shields held high. The order to advance rang out from their officers.

I stood and walked into the empty space before the army. 'Halt your advance, and turn your army, king!' I shouted. 'You will not rule here.'

I pulled my knife from my belt and held it high above my head.

This caused some hesitancy in the front line of soldiers. Were they all expected to attack one girl holding one knife? Their officers urged them forward.

As confusion reigned in the ranks of the king's army, Little Bear emerged from the forest, followed by every wild bear on the island. Holding a line behind Little Bear, they advanced onto the sea ice. Once there, Little Bear stood on her hind legs and let out a roar that echoed around the bay, into the forests behind and all the way to the mountains.

It were more than a threat. It were a summons.

Soon the land was alive with movement, every creature responding to Little Bear's roar, called by the trees to come and drive back the king's invading force.

Behind the bears were the dogs, lead out of the forest by Poke. There were all manner of sizes and colours in the company, and I thought I caught a glimpse of the pack that had lived around the miners' camp and used to be both my foes and friends. They had the broad brows and heavy-set chests of dogs used to surviving by their wits.

Behind the dogs were the donkeys and even some billy goats, long horns waving menacingly, come to lend what assistance they might.

And flying above, a thick cloud of birds. My funeral choir, led by the falcon, appearing once again to sing for me.

The king's army faltered. They'd been willing enough to fight men in exchange for their meagre pay packets, but they found they weren't being paid enough to clash with bears and dogs.

Little Bear had her troops paw the ice and bare their teeth but as fierce as they looked, we dint have the king's army on the run just yet.

Officers bawled their orders, and the king's line held.

The hunter swung his rifle into his hands and fired one shot into the air. It broke through all the noise and confusion of the shuffling army and there was a moment of silence.

The huge flock of birds in the sky above seemed to pause in mid-flight, and then they swooped.

In a black mass of squawking and shrieking, they descended on the army, knocking off helmets and carrying them away, and forcing the soldiers to drop to the ground and cover their heads with their arms.

Some soldiers began running away, and Rose Red put out a flag saying the line was breaking.

'We're not done yet,' I said, and dropped to one knee to tap my knife on the ice.

At my signal, another dense black cloud rose from the sand of the beach and approached the king's army. Again the king's officers could not maintain discipline. The soldiers shifted nervously, some of them kneeling, some turning to run away. Some started praying to their god, believing the cloud to be a demon. There was bellowing from inside the king's carriage as he realised his army's resolve was faltering.

The black cloud was worse than whatever evil magic they'd imagined. It flew toward the army, falling on it in a biting, stinging mass. Not one soldier could abide the nipping of the midges and they fled screaming across the ice. Not even the king was immune. The insects flew through the cracks in his sealed carriage and fell on him in droves.

One last thing. I turned to Lady where she perched on my basket and she launched into flight, crying out.

While the midges swarmed, causing chaos among the troops, an army of rats emerged from the forest cover and ran out over the ice. Falling on the leather harnesses of the animals enslaved to haul the war machines and the king's sled, the rats nibbled them free. Their harnesses fell to the ice and the beasts stepped out of them gratefully. The newly liberated horses and donkeys, freed of their heavy burdens, trotted toward the beach and disappeared under the trees. The killing machines they'd dropped sat heavily on the ice with no possible return to the king's empire.

Their job done, the rats dispersed. To my relief, it had to be said.

Officers ordered men to pick up the shafts of the king's sled to pull it, in place of the horses that had gaily departed.

I shouted after my grandfather. 'Remember, king, if you ever return, the very land will rise up to repel you. You've felt it now, your rule is not welcome here. Go now and never return.'

Finishing my speech, and feeling not a little silly for shouting to the backs of a retreating army, the hunter and I climbed into our baskets and launched our balloons, rising to watch the army's retreat and ensure it stayed that way. The birds and the midges kept up their harassment, but there was no need for Little Bear and Poke's troops. They had not been needed, mercies granted, and returned to their business in the forest.

Dog-boy and Rose Red

Rose Red and Dog-boy were married as the long days shortened. Neither were sure how old they were exactly. Still young but old enough to know their minds and their devotion to each other. I gave my approval not because they needed it but because they asked me for it sweetly. They told me they thought of me like their older sister, which were flattering but I couldn't stop from bursting out, *Not that much older!* to save my pride. Wedding preparations went side-by-side with those for the long nights. I was making sure everyone knew this storm season would be harder than we'd had before. The better we prepared, the more likely we'd last it out. It was hard and grim work. Building walls high and strong, mortaring every crack and cranny to keep them tight against icy drafts. Repairing and shoring up roofs, weaving curtains and beds and warm clothing for everyone. Cook's kitchen were in business night and day, the old stove getting white-hot as it baked and dried and stewed and boiled and simmered all manner of produce for the pantries.

Dog-boy's latest obsession was reading the weather and forecasting what was coming using instruments he'd made himself based on what he'd learned from Memma. He told us it would be the worst of the worst we'd ever seen. If it were that bad for us, then at least we were safe from the old king, my grandfather, rallying another army. That was some comfort.

Dog-boy still nursed the wound of Memma's betrayal but he was determined to hold on to what he'd learned from her, and not let it be tainted by the shame of how he'd been used. How we'd all been used. We waited for fire-mountain's next mood. I hoped for its fires to start to cool, for its temper to quieten, for the hot gas to burn itself out. Knowing now, though I'd known it before, and no one believed me, that there was nothing anyone could do to change this. It weren't going to be me or anyone else lifting the clouds. It would be fire-mountain, when it was burnt through. The volcano would quieten of its own accord. The king across the sea in the Restoration lands had his own opinion, of course. However we waited, we would endure whatever we had to. We would survive.

Having a wedding alongside all the hard work was something to look forward to for everyone. We chose a calm bright day and the whole chateau assembled in the freshly swept bailey. Rose Red had refused to use valuable daylight on the looms to make her dress, instead sewing it late in the evenings. Of course it was a ruby-red gown, sprinkled with snow-white flowers, with a lace hood covering her fiery hair. Dog-boy wore a gold waistcoat that fitted him perfectly and matched Poke's golden coat. The dog had been bathed and brushed until he was twice the size in fluff and smiling proudly.

Mister teacher said some words at the ceremony and while he spoke I looked over at the hunter. He smiled at me, showing his crooked teeth. *Maybe we should've done a ceremony,* I thought. And maybe it weren't too late. But this was a day for Rose Red and Dog-boy and all the fun of celebrating being alive. There was food to eat and dancing in the great hall and falling into bed at a late hour feeling happy, even though life was far from easy.

As I worked alongside the rest of the chateau family, my mind wandered. One day, scrubbing floors, I sat back on my heels in amazement. I knew who I was, where I'd come from. It weren't all good news, that was for sure, but knowing it had silenced that part of me that was always wondering. Now I knew who I was, it mattered, and it mattered not at all. I were me, Snow, and I were here right now, scrubbing brush in my hand and acres of floor yet to be cleaned. I regretted having a grandfather who were so cruel he killed my father to spite my mother, and my heart broke for her, running away with her grief and then dying alone. But she'd delivered me into safe hands. Though I'd had my own struggles, now I had my chateau family, human and animal, and I was exactly who I wanted to be. Princess Snow or plain Snow, still there were floors to be scrubbed. I dipped my brush in the sudsy water and got back to work.

Acknowledgements

I would like to acknowledge, with respect, that I am a recent arrival in Aotearoa, New Zealand, and as a writer I have no right to speak on that which I don't understand. All mistakes are my own. I acknowledge Māori as tangata whenua and strive to honour te Tiriti. All my love and thanks as always to Ben and my daughters Asha and Milla. To my teeny tiny writers group, Nishanie and Susannah, thank you for all the supportive Sundays. To everyone at Wakefield Press, thank you for your unflagging generosity and book-related wisdom, especially Maddy Sexton for her editing, Jonathon Inverarity for always knowing where everything is, and Michael Bollen for his unfaltering dedication to all the books. My gratitude as well to the trees, for their therapeutic wonder and for making the paper.

www.ingramcontent.com/pod-product-compliance
Lightning Source LLC
Chambersburg PA
CBHW020600030726
47497CB00007B/2034